HER BLUEGRASS BEAU

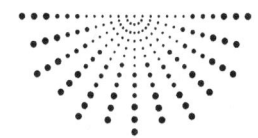

CAROL PREFLATISH

STARDUST ROMANCE

ISBN: 978-1-942212-92-8

Stardust Romance Publishing
Goshen, Kentucky 40026
Stardustromance.com

For my Kentucky friends.

CHAPTER ONE

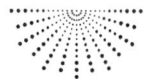

"It's over with Brent. I don't ever want to see him again, and I told him that too," Karri said, explaining her recent breakup to her best friend, Alexandria. "I'm tired of being treated like I'm his servant."

"You don't really mean that. You two have been seeing each other far too long to end it like that."

"Three years? Three years isn't that long." She got up from the kitchen table to get a bottle of water from the refrigerator. "Want one?" she asked, holding up a bottle.

Alex shook her head no, and Karri sat back down at the table and opened her bottle for a sip.

"If you're serious about not getting back together, you should get right back in the dating scene. Let's go to that new comedy club tonight," Alex suggested.

"I need more than that. I need to get away for a while. A vacation, that's it, I need a vacation-- alone."

"A week off from the bookstore might be just what you need."

"I don't mean just stay home. I need to get out of Los Angeles, and it would be for more than a week."

"Where did you have in mind?"

"Well, actually I was thinking Kentucky."

Alex gave her a confused look. "Kentucky?"

"My great-aunt Alma, from Kentucky, passed away several months ago. Her husband passed away about thirty years before, and they didn't have any children. I remember going with my parents to visit on her farm when I was young."

"Karri, I'm so sorry. I didn't know about your loss."

"Thanks. I didn't mention it to anyone. I only visited her a few times, and I was pretty young, but her farm was just the best place for a kid to hang out. Anyway, I recently received a letter from her attorney saying she left me her farm and a little money."

"Wow, a farm," Alex teased.

"He said that there are some papers that I need to sign, and I was going to ask him to mail them to me, but I think I'll take a little time off from the bookstore and fly out to the farm for a few weeks."

Alex broke out into hysterical laughter. "You on a farm?"

"Stop laughing."

"I'm sorry," Alex said, wiping tears from her eyes. "But, the thought of a city girl like you on a farm is just too funny."

"It's not a working farm. Aunt Alma hasn't had any farming done there in years."

"And, how do you know that?"

"I spoke with the attorney on the phone yesterday. Actually, I'm planning on putting the place up for sale, and I'd like to take a last look at it at least before I do. The attorney suggested that I go through Aunt Alma's things before deciding what to do with the place."

"I suppose a trip like that would be a good distraction from Brent," Alex said. "When do you plan to go?"

"I think I'll leave next Saturday. That should give me enough time to arrange for my absence at the store."

"At least with owning your own bookstore, you don't have to worry about not being able to get off work."

"Yes, Millie can handle the store for a few weeks, and I can have a nice little vacation."

Five days later, Karri was on a plane headed to Kentucky. After six hours of flying with one layover, she arrived at the Lexington Airport, the closest to Willow Creek, Kentucky where her Aunt Alma had lived. It was six o'clock in the evening when she landed and already dark outside. She quickly retrieved her luggage and went to the car rental counter to pick up her car. After getting all the paperwork signed, she got to the car and punched the address into the GPS. At the exit of the airport, she saw the *Welcome to Kentucky - The Bluegrass State* sign. She let out a deep breath and was on her way to Willow Creek. "This could be an adventure," she said to herself.

Twenty minutes after exiting off of the interstate highway, she reached the small town of Willow Creek. Driving through the town as the GPS instructed, it kept recalculating. Apparently, the device didn't know where the farm was either.

She pulled into a parking lot and got out the directions from the attorney. After reading through them, she left town and then five miles outside of town turned north onto a road that was becoming narrower as she drove. She wondered if two cars could even pass each other. As she continued her journey, she felt as if she was heading into a black hole. The countryside was pitch black.

Karri stopped the car along the side of the road for a few minutes and turned on the map light. She rechecked the driving instructions and was sure she was close to her destination.

Slowly, she drove up a small hill and came to a split in the road. She took the road to the right hoping it was the correct one. When she saw three mailboxes, she knew she was near the farm. Turning at the mailboxes, the road became narrower again, if that was even possible. She saw three driveways but wasn't sure which one was for her aunt's house. The directions didn't specify. She chose the second driveway and finally stopped in front of a house. There was a light on inside, so she knew she had chosen wrong. Instead of going back to one of the other roads, she decided to ask the person at this house for directions.

She got out of the car pulled the collar of her coat closed at her neck to keep the cold February air out. As she walked up the sidewalk, she could see that it was a big log house. There was no doorbell and when she knocked on the door, the barking of what sounded like a vicious dog inside startled her. She jumped back when the dog appeared in a full-length window alongside the front door.

"Colt, quiet!" a male voice said from inside. The porch light came on and the door opened. "Can I help you?"

The glare from the inside light made it hard to see the man clearly behind the screen in the door. "I'm looking for Alma Carter's place. Am I anywhere close to it?" she asked.

"What business do you have there?" His voice was deep, and she wished she could see his face.

"I'm her great-niece, and I've come to spend a few weeks on the farm."

"Are you Karri?" he asked, his voice softened.

"Yes, Karri Taylor. How did you know?"

"James Gilmore told me you were coming. Please come in, you must be freezing." He opened the door inviting her inside.

She hesitated, not sure if she should come inside or not. First, there was that dog she heard; and second, the man was a stranger.

"It's okay. We're neighbors. Alma's farm is just back the road there. Please come in and warm up a bit."

Karri didn't know why, but she decided to trust him and entered the house looking around for the dog.

"I'm Jake Duncan, and this is my dog, Colt."

Karri didn't move. The dog was suddenly next to Jake. She thought he looked a little like a German Shepard but wasn't sure since she didn't know much about dogs.

"He won't bite. He sounds mean, but he really isn't. Come here, Colt. Meet Alma's niece."

The dog walked slowing over to Karri and sat at her feet.

"I'm not a big fan of dogs." She looked up at Jake finally getting a good look at him. He was tall with broad shoulders and dark brown wavy hair with a stubble of beard growing on his face. His eyes, there was something about his eyes, very dark and sexy. He was a very handsome man, she thought.

"Go lay down," he ordered the dog and then turned back to Karri. "Would you like some coffee?"

"No, thank you. I really should get to the house."

"Of course, I'm sorry. If you turn left at the end of my driveway and go straight back, you'll end up right at her house. It's the only house back there."

"Thank you." She turned to leave and he reached around to open the door for her.

"Do you have a key to the house?" he asked.

"Mr. Gilmore told me where he hid one so I could get in tonight."

"Would you like for me to follow you back there to make sure you get inside okay?"

She walked out onto the porch. "No, thank you. I'm from Los Angeles. If you live there, you can handle just about anything."

She noticed he tried to hide a laugh when she said that and thought that was a little rude. There was no way she was going to let him follow her to a secluded house in an area that she didn't know that well. "Thank you for your help."

"If you need anything, just let me know."

She gave him a little wave as she walked back to her car. Backing down Jake's driveway, she turned the car around and turned left as he had instructed. Not far, she found the farmhouse. The key was on top of a beam on the porch roof, just as the attorney said. The door opened with a creek and she walked inside. She found the light switch on the left and turned the lights on.

Vague memories of being in this house came back to her. The wooden staircase on the left side of the living room led up to several bedrooms on the second floor. The living room in front of her had a beautiful old rocking chair next to a big fireplace in the middle of one of the walls. Karri closed and locked the door. The house was cold, and she spotted a thermostat on the wall and walked over to turn on the furnace. Then, she headed past the staircase to the kitchen in the rear of the house. Other than a little dust, it was as if great-aunt Alma had never left as everything was still in place. A small dining table was against one of the walls. The counters were clear, except for a basket that Karri remembered always held fruit from the Alma's trees in the backyard. Pots hung on the wall and a broom leaned by the door in the corner.

Karri noticed that the refrigerator was running. She was almost afraid to open it, hoping it didn't have spoiled food inside. Luckily, she found it empty. The freezer was empty as well, except for a couple of ice trays, but then she noticed that there was no coffeemaker or microwave on the counter. It was then she realized how hungry she was. Her stomach was beginning to emit hunger sounds and there was no food in the house. How could she have forgotten to stop to get some take-out on her way from the airport? Out here in nowhere land, she knew there'd be no deliveries.

She went back out to the rental car and brought her suitcases inside and dug through her carry-on bag pulling out a couple of protein bars. She opened the cabinet doors until she found the drinking glasses. She filled a glass with water from the tap and ice from the freezer. "This will have to do for dinner." Tomorrow, she would find a supermarket to get some groceries for her visit. She took a seat at the table and unwrapped the protein bars and sipped on the ice water. After her meal, she looked through the kitchen cabinets to do a quick inventory before heading to the store tomorrow. She definitely wanted to get a coffeemaker. The bathroom was just as bare as the kitchen, but at least it was stocked with toilet paper.

Before heading up the stairs, she turned the thermostat up to seventy-two. She pulled her large suitcase up the stairs and found the master bedroom on the right. It reminded her of a bed and breakfast room that she and Brent had stayed in at Big Bear Lake, California. The bed itself was nothing fancy, but the bedspread looked to be an old handmade quilt, probably stitched by Aunt Alma herself she thought as she ran her hand over it. The room was decorated with little figurines of angels on the tables and paintings hanging on two of the walls, with a mirror on another. The fourth wall had a large bookcase filled with novels of all types on it.

Karri put her clothes away and dressed for bed. The old house still felt cold to her. She was more accustomed to the warmer temperatures of her hometown of Costa Mesa. She found a blanket in the dresser and unfolded it placing it on top of the bed. She scanned the bookcase for something to read before going to sleep. She chose a Zane Grey western, and after blowing the dust off of it, she crawled into bed. She wished she had a cup of hot tea right now and made a mental note to add that to a list for the market first thing in the morning. After her long flight, it didn't take long for Karri to fall asleep.

The next morning, she woke up thinking she heard a noise. There it was again. Someone was pounding on the front door. Still dark outside, she looked at her watch that showed seven o'clock local time. She quickly got out of bed, grabbed her robe and headed down the stairs to the door. Before opening it, she looked around for something to protect herself. She spotted an umbrella behind the door and picked it up. It would have to do. She turned the porch light on and moved the curtain on the door aside to see who was waking her up at such an early hour. It was four a.m. in California.

Standing on the other side of the door was Jake, the neighbor she met last night. "Good morning," his frosty breath floated upward as he spoke.

"What do you want?" she said, still not opening the door.

"I brought you some coffee and biscuits with sorghum. Can I come in? It's kind of cold out here."

Karri looked up at the big round thermometer that hung from the porch roof and saw the temperature was nineteen degrees. The thought of that hot coffee sounded too good to pass up, especially since her bare feet were freezing. She opened the door to let Jake inside and pulled her light robe around her. She shivered when the cold air hit her skin.

"Thanks. The cold was beginning to make it through my clothes." He immediately started walking toward the kitchen. He held a thermos in one hand and a pie tin with aluminum foil over it. More rudeness, she thought. She put the umbrella back and followed him to the kitchen.

"I figured you didn't have any food here and would be hungry for breakfast. I fixed me some biscuits this morning and thought I'd bring

7

some back to you." He turned on the oven and uncovered the pie tin of biscuits. From one coat pocket, he sat a glass jar of brown syrupy looking substance on the table and then from the other pocket, he took out a small piece of aluminum foil. When he unfolded it, she saw it had butter inside.

"You think of everything, don't you?"

"I try. Why don't get a couple plates and coffee cups for us. I only brought some sugar, I hope you don't use cream?" He took a plastic zipper bag of sugar out of the same pocket that had held the butter.

"Sugar is fine." She went to the cabinet and got some plates and cups. After rinsing and drying them, she brought them to the table. Jake got silverware from one of the drawers and placed them on the table.

He sure knows his way around this kitchen, she thought. As he poured her a cup of coffee, she thought she might be salivating. She added two sugars to her cup and took a long drink before sitting down.

"Take it easy, that's hot."

"No, it's perfect," she said, after swallowing.

Back at the stove, Jake checked the oven and it was ready to put the biscuits in. "It shouldn't take long for them to warm up."

"If you don't mind, I'm going to go change into some warmer clothes," she said.

"I don't blame you. You sure don't look like you came too prepared for a Kentucky winter."

Karri left the kitchen and went upstairs to put on some sweatpants and a sweater. When she came back down, Jake was checking on the biscuits in the oven. She sat at the table. "You seem to know your way around my aunt's kitchen pretty well."

He joined Karri at the table. "I used to stop by often to check on her. With her having no family around, a few of us neighbors took it upon ourselves to make sure she was okay, had plenty of food, and that the house was warm enough, things like that."

Karri wasn't sure, but she thought he had just insulted her with his comment about family. "My mother told me once that she and my father tried several times to get Aunt Alma to move in with them in California, but she always refused."

Jake laughed. "That sounds like Alma. She loved living here, and I'm not surprised she didn't want to leave. She was pretty set in her ways and wouldn't ever want to feel like a burden to anyone."

"Yet, she let neighbors look after her?"

"She didn't think of it that way. Believe me, when she was able, she took care of us too. During the holidays, she baked pies and cakes for all of us and there wasn't a Sunday at church that she didn't have homemade cookies for the kids." Jake got up to check the biscuits.

When he opened the oven door, the aroma of freshly baked biscuits drifted past her and she then realized how hungry she was. He brought them over to the table and placed the pan down on top of a towel. Jake opened the jar of the brown syrupy liquid and poured some on both plates. She watched as he buttered his biscuit before dipping it in the thick brown liquid, and taking a bite.

"What is that?"

"Sorghum. You've never had sorghum?"

"I've never heard of it."

"Sorghum is sort of like molasses, but made from a plant that looks like corn in the fields. Where are you from again?"

"Costa Mesa, California. It's near Los Angeles."

"Oh."

"What do you mean, oh?" she asked, mocking him.

"You're from the city. If you stay here for very long, you're going to have to learn about country living."

"I don't plan on being here that long, but if I were, I can assure you, I could take care of myself very well."

He didn't respond, except to get up to leave. "I'll come back later to pick up my thermos and pie pan. Keep the sorghum. I guess you're going to need to get some groceries since you've got nothing in the house. I wrote down the directions to the store." He handed her a piece of paper.

She looked at the directions. "Thanks, but why would you do this for me?"

"Why? We're neighbors and neighbors do things for each other."

He put his coat on and walked out of the kitchen. Karri followed him to the door. He stopped before stepping out into the cold. "If you need anything, my phone number is at the bottom of that paper. There's no phone here, but I figured you've probably got a cell phone."

"Yes, I do. Thank you for the coffee. Oh, and next time you decide to stop by, could you at least wait until daylight?" She smiled at him.

"Sorry. Everyone around here gets up with the chickens."

Karri closed the door behind him and watched as he walked to his truck and drove back up the long driveway.

Nice looking guy, she thought. She decided she needed another biscuit and more coffee. With only the protein bars for dinner last night, she was very hungry. She even tried some of the sorghum he left. It tasted a little sweet with just a touch of bitterness, but she liked it.

The clock on the wall now showed eight o'clock, still too early to call Alex back in California. After she finished her breakfast and washed the dishes, she went back upstairs to change her clothes for the day. Once she was back in the kitchen, she made a list of groceries before picking up Jake's directions for the store and heading out the door.

The sun was up and shining brightly now, but even that didn't keep the property from looking glum. Everything looked so brown. Winter in the south was definitely not colorful.

She got into the car and headed up the driveway. Even with all the brown, everything looked much better than it did when she arrived in the darkness of the night before. Once she reached the top of the hill, Jake's log house came into view. It was beautiful with lots of pine trees around the yard and a split rail fence that she hadn't noticed last night. That's when she realized that it wasn't just a cabin on a small farm, but a log home on a large farm with horses and cattle in the pastures around the barn. A little farther down the road, she found Jake standing next to his truck. It looked like he was working on the fence along the pasture. She thought about stopping but decided it best not to. She also had an appointment with her aunt's attorney to get to. He waved as she drove by and she returned the gesture.

Jake's directions were very good and Karri found the market in town with no problem. She wasn't sure she would call the store a supermarket because it was much smaller than the stores in California. It still had all the same departments, but on a smaller scale. One thing she did notice was that the market had no alcohol for sale. Not that she really needed it, but she thought it would be nice to give Jake a bottle of wine in return for the breakfast this morning.

After loading the groceries and the coffee maker she bought into her car, she drove through town in search of the attorney's office. That's when she saw a liquor store at the corner of the block.

She parked on the street and went inside. It was a small store with only two aisles of wine, but was thrilled to find a bottle of good California wine. After completing her purchase of two bottles and a corkscrew that she was sure Aunt Alma wouldn't have, she went back to the car and found the attorney's office only a few blocks away.

"James Gilmore, Attorney at Law." She read the sign to herself and then opened the door to the office.

"May I help you?" the secretary asked.

"I'm Karri Taylor, here to see Mr. Gilmore about Alma Carter's estate."

The secretary checked the appointment book and glanced at her telephone. "He's on the phone right now. If you'll have a seat in the waiting area, he'll be right with you."

Karri took a seat. The room was decorated with a mauve colored carpet with the walls a lighter shade. Coordinated silk flower arrangements adorned the tables. A variety of magazines ranging from farming to basketball to national news were also on the tables. Karri had just opened a magazine when she heard her name.

"Miss Taylor." She stood up. "I'm James Gilmore, won't you please come into my office?" They shook hands, and she followed him into another room.

"Please, sit down. I was rather surprised when I received your e-mail saying you were coming to Kentucky. I thought you would handle everything over the phone and through the mail."

"I needed a vacation and wanted to see the farm one more time before the sale. I haven't been here since I was a child."

"You are still planning on selling it, correct?" He opened a legal-size folder with several papers in it.

"Yes, I am. I have no intention to keep it."

"Very good. There are a couple ways of selling it. We can list it with a real estate agent, or we can auction it."

"I don't know much about either way. Which do you recommend?"

"Both have advantages and disadvantages. Putting it in the hands of real estate agent might get you a little more money because you can negotiate the price with the prospective buyer, but it could take a bit longer to sell. With an auction, it's going to sell right then, but possibly at a lesser price."

"I think I'd like to let a real estate agent handle the sale. I like the idea of negotiating. Can you take care of securing an agent?"

"Yes, I can take care of that today." He made a few notes in the file on his desk. "I believe I previously mentioned to you that Alma left you a sum of money."

"Yes, but not how much."

"The balance of her liquid assets comes to around $80,000, and of course, you will get the proceeds from the sale of the farm after expenses."

The hair stood up on the back of Karri's neck. "I had no idea it would be so much."

Your great-aunt received a good income from her late husband's pension, as well as her own Social Security check. She rarely spent money, saving it instead. I suspect that farm will bring well over three-hundred thousand dollars if we can find the right buyer."

"Do you think it will be hard finding someone to buy it?"

"The economy is down right now. It's not something just anyone can afford to buy. On the other hand, the farm is in a good location and because of that, is worth a good price."

"I see. Well, I trust you can find a suitable real estate agent to find a buyer."

"I think I can."

"Is there anything I need to sign before I go?"

"How long do you plan on staying here before heading back to California?"

"I'll be here for about two weeks."

"I will have some papers for you to sign and I'll need to know what kind of transaction you want to do in order to deposit the money."

"Oh, I hadn't thought about that.

"Do you have an accountant?" he asked.

Karri laughed. "There's a company that I use for my business, but they don't handle any of my personal finances."

"I recommend hiring an accountant and have him set up some accounts that the money can be directly deposited into. I will continue to hold the money here until you can get that done." He scribbled more notes in the file.

"I will do that as soon as I return home. Is there anything else that I need to do?"

"I think that just about does it. I'll call you when the paperwork is ready for your signature. I don't believe there's a phone at your great-aunt's house now, do you have a cell phone?"

"Yes, you should have my number on file."

Gilmore looked at the first page in the folder. "Yes, here it is." He stood up and extended his hand. "It was very nice to meet you. I'm sure this will be a smooth process."

"Thank you. Please let me know if you need anything else."

He walked her out to the front lobby and then took another waiting client back as she went out the door.

Karri checked her watch. It was near noon, and she felt hungry. She looked around and wondered if there was somewhere to eat around here. The day was cold enough that the groceries in her car were safe from spoiling, so she got in and went in search of a restaurant. It didn't take long to find one about three blocks down the street and one block over. *Gracie's Place*, it said on the sign.

She went inside and sat at a booth next to a window. A young waitress came over and handed her a menu.

"Our special today is fried fish, macaroni and cheese, and corn. Can I take your drink order?"

"Ice water with some lemon, please," she answered.

She thought about the special of the day but decided it had too many carbs. The restaurant was small in relation to the ones Karri frequented back home. She wondered if Jake ever ate here. It would be nice if he would walk in and share lunch with her. At that moment, the bell hanging on the door dinged. She was almost afraid to look over at the door, fearing her wish might come true. Taking a chance glance over, she saw it wasn't Jake, but another man dressed as though he had just left work at the farm for lunch.

A terrible thought popped into Karri's head. What if he's married? She didn't see a wife at his house the other night, but his wife might have sent him down with breakfast this morning.

When the waitress brought her drink, she had made her decision for lunch. "I'll have a grilled chicken salad with ranch dressing."

"Thanks. You aren't from around here, are ya?" the waitress said with a southern drawl.

"No, I'm not."

"Are ya here visiting family or something?"

"My great-aunt passed away and I am here taking care of some business for her."

"I'm sorry to hear that. Who was she?"

"I doubt you would know her."

"You'd be surprised. I know most people around here."

"Her name was Alma Carter."

"Miss Alma, why yes I knew her. She was a grand lady. We went to the same church. I'm sorry for your loss."

"Thank you, but I didn't really know her very well. I hadn't seen her since I was young."

"That's too bad. You'd have loved Miss Alma."

"You called her Miss Alma. Why? She wasn't a Miss."

"She was my Sunday School teacher when I was little. All the kids

14

called her Miss Alma. She was like a grandma to all of us." The wait-ress then left to take the lunch order to the kitchen.

Karri was intrigued to learn that her great-aunt was a Sunday School teacher. She wondered what other interesting things about Alma she'd learn.

CHAPTER TWO

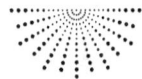

After lunch, Karri drove back to the farmhouse, and when she turned onto the last road to the house, she saw Jake standing at the mailbox and decided to do the neighborly thing this time and stop to talk. She rolled down the car window. "Hi."

"Hello. I see you went grocery shopping," he said, looking at the back seat of the car.

"Yes, thanks for the directions. I found the store pretty easy."

"Glad to help."

There was an awkward moment of silence. She looked at his hand for a wedding ring, but he was wearing gloves on this cold February day. Finally, Karri gathered up the courage to ask what was on her mind. "Would you and your wife like to come to dinner this evening?"

He hesitated before answering. "Ah, I'm not married."

"Oh, I'm sorry. I didn't know."

"No problem, but thanks for asking anyway."

"So, you don't want to come for dinner?" she questioned.

"You still want me to?"

"I do. I want to repay you for bringing breakfast this morning."

A smile spread across his face. "What time should I be there?"

"How about eight?"

"Eight?" He looked confused.

"Is that a bad time?"

"Most people around here eat supper around six."

"Supper? Is that the same as dinner?"

Jake cracked a smile. "Yeah, that would be the same as dinner to you."

"You're making fun of me, aren't you?" She tilted her head to the side in a flirtatious move.

"No, ma'am. I would never do that." He laughed.

"Come at six, then. I hope you like grilled chicken and baked vegetables."

"Sounds great. Can I bring something?"

"Oh, no. You don't need to bring anything.

"Are you sure? I feel bad coming empty-handed."

"Positive."

"Okay. I'll be there at six."

Karri smiled as she put the window up and drove on to the house. She would need to get the place tidied up since it had been vacant for so long and get dinner started if she was to have everything ready by six. She'd been so busy since arriving she hadn't had time even to dust the house.

She unloaded the groceries from the car and put them away. Before she started cleaning, she had one thing to do.

"Hi Alex, it's Karri," she said into her cell phone.

"Karri, how's farm life in mid-America?"

"Actually, it's not so bad. It's kind of nice in the country. I just wish it were warmer." She sat down on the couch, kicked off her shoes, and put her feet up.

"How cold is it?"

"It was in the thirties today, but so much colder last night."

"Glad it's you and not me. Hey, any good-looking men out there?"

"You have only one thing on your mind." Karri laughed. "Well, there is this one neighbor."

"Neighbor? Wow, next door, eh? How convenient."

"Neighbors aren't exactly next door out here, but he does live up the road. His name is Jake, and he's a farmer."

It was Alex's turn to laugh now. It sounded like she had dropped the phone from laughing so hard.

"Alex? Alex?"

"Farmer? You're hot for a farmer? I can't wait to tell the girls at spinning class about the city girl and the farmer."

"Very funny. I'm so glad you're getting such a good laugh out of this."

"Okay, okay. Tell me about your farmer," Alex said, still snickering.

"I met him last night when I arrived. I couldn't find Aunt Alma's farm and stopped by his house to ask for directions. Then, he came by this morning with breakfast because he knew I didn't have any food in the house. He's tall, has broad shoulders, sandy colored hair, and gorgeous brown eyes. He's built like some of those construction workers we used to watch across the street from the bookstore."

"Sounds interesting. Does this mean you're not coming home to California ever again?"

"No, it's nice here, but the quietness is driving me crazy, and the fresh air is killing my lungs," Karri said, laughing. "I'm suffering in this cold weather too."

"Oh, but you have a farm boy to keep you warm."

"I'm having him over for dinner tonight."

"Really? You're sure not wasting any time. I want to hear all about it tomorrow."

"I'm just returning his kindness of bringing me breakfast this morning, nothing more. I better go. I need to clean the house a little and start cooking dinner."

"Okay. Don't forget to call me tomorrow with details. Have a great night."

"Bye." Karri hung up her cell phone.

The house really wasn't dirty. It only needed a little dusting and the carpet vacuumed. Her designer clothes and shoes weren't exactly the type of clothes to wear when cleaning house. Before changing clothes, she put one of the bottles of wine in the refrigerator to chill and marinated some boneless chicken breasts.

She headed upstairs to put on a pair of jeans and a long-sleeved T-shirt and then came back downstairs where she found the vacuum cleaner in the kitchen closet. After quickly going over the carpet in the living room, she dusted the tables and then the shelf over the fire-place. In one of the bags from the grocery store, she brought out several pine-scented candles. This should help the house smell a little better, she thought as she lit one candle placing it on the mantle in the living room.

The bathroom was next to be cleaned. She brought an air fresh-ener, and after twisting it open, she placed it on the shelf above the towels. The green color of the air freshener matched the color scheme in the room perfect. The pattern on the wallpaper was household plants on a white background, and she thought the yellow painted ceiling symbolized the sun. Karri liked the sun, and she liked that her great aunt had chosen that color. She put out some fresh towels and finished by putting a new bar of soap in the dish.

The last thing before starting on dinner was to straighten up the bedroom. She laughed at herself because she knew there would be no action in there tonight. Although, she had fantasized he'd be fantastic in bed. She smoothed out the bedspread and fluffed the pillows before laying them at the head of the bed. The floors were hardwood, and she went back downstairs to get a dust mop for the bedroom floor. Lastly, she placed a new candle on the tables on each side of the bed.

She had worked up quite a sweat doing all this housecleaning and wanted to take a quick shower before he got there. From the closet, she chose blue slacks and floral print blouse to wear. Before stepping into the bathroom, she grabbed her shampoo and vanilla scented shower gel from her bag.

When she entered the upstairs bathroom, she found no shower, but only an old fashion clawfoot bathtub. She knew the downstairs bathroom didn't have a shower either so this would have to do. After undressing, she turned the brass cross handles on the faucet to let the warm water flow into the tub. Testing the temperature with her toe first, she eased down into the water. "Oh, this feels so good. I could soak here for hours," she said to herself.

Twenty minutes later, the water was beginning to get cold, and she realized the time. Karri put on her terry cloth robe after drying off, went into the bedroom to get her hair dryer and stood in front of the mirror to dry her long hair. Makeup was next. Some eyeliner, mascara, and a little lipstick and her face looked perfect. She got dressed and headed back to the kitchen.

She put on an apron to keep her clothes clean and turned on the radio trying to find a classic rock station, but settled on country music. The chicken breasts had marinated long enough, and it was time to put them in the oven. She listened to the news on the radio as she put the finishing touches on dinner. Lots of stories about arrests and auto accidents, then the local obituaries were read. Finally, they gave the weather report.

Tonight's weather will be cloudy with temps around 30 degrees. A low-pressure system will be moving through the region with snow developing by morning. Accumulations should be an inch or less.

"Oh boy, snow." she said out loud to herself. She hadn't seen snow since her skiing trip to Utah four years ago. She couldn't wait.

A glance at the clock showed five-thirty. He would be there soon. She had to hurry, so she started chopping the green beans, peppers, onions, zucchini, and yellow squash into a baking dish. A drizzle of olive oil, with a dash of salt and pepper, and after a quick stir, she placed the dish next to the chicken in the oven. Both entrees should be done at the same time.

I've got just enough time to mix the salad, and I should be ready, she thought to herself.

At six o'clock on the dot, there was a knock at the door. "Oh no, he's here already."

She removed her apron and checked herself in the mirror to make sure everything was in place. Her long brown hair was straight and fell below her shoulders. The colors in the blouse enhanced her brown eyes. She took a deep breath and went to open the door.

"Hi. I'm glad you could make it," she said. He looked gorgeous dressed in a brown plaid flannel shirt and blue jeans. His face was clean-shaven, and his aftershave smelled wonderful.

"I brought these for you." He handed her a bouquet of fresh, colorful flowers.

"Thank you. They're beautiful. Oh, I'm sorry, please come in. It's too cold to stand in the doorway."

Jake stepped inside and removed his coat, hanging it on the hook by the door. "Something sure smells good."

"Please come in, and I'll get you something to drink. Dinner, or rather supper as you call it, should be ready soon."

Jake followed her into the kitchen. Karri opened the refrigerator door. "I hope you like wine."

"Yes, I do."

She brought the bottle of wine, two goblets, and the corkscrew to the table where they sat down. "You'll have to forgive me for the goblets. I couldn't find any wine glasses here. Would you mind opening the bottle for me?"

"Not all. Happy to help. Alma wouldn't have any wine glasses here. She never wanted any alcohol in the house." She handed the bottle and corkscrew to him. "Oh, a California wine," he said.

"Is something wrong with that? Some of the best wines in the world are from California."

In no time, Jake had the bottle open and began filling the glasses. "You know, we have a very good winery just down the road a few miles. They've won several awards for their wines." He handed her a glass.

"Really? I may have to check it out before I go home." She waited until he took the first sip. "How is it?"

"Not bad. I like it."

She let out a deep breath. "Good, because I have a bottle of it for you to take home in return for the breakfast."

"I thought that's what this meal was for."

"I owe you a lot. I was starved this morning."

Jake laughed. "I doubt you would have passed out from malnourishment."

A buzzer on the stove sounded and she went over to remove the chicken placing the pan on top of the stove.

"That smells great. Can I help with anything?"

"There's some vegetables still in the oven, can you get those out while I take the salad into the dining room."

Jake grabbed a towel and took the vegetables out, too. "Where do you want them?"

"On the table in here," she called from the dining room. "There's already a towel to sit them on."

While he took the vegetables into the other room, she came back in to get the platter with the chicken breasts and followed him in.

"I'll get the wine," she said, after setting down the platter.

"No, you sit, and I'll get the wine." He stood behind one of the chairs waiting for her to sit. She moved over and sat down while he held the chair for her. He then stepped back into the kitchen and brought out the bottle and both glasses.

He took his seat and lifted the chicken platter holding it toward her so she could serve herself first, then he put a piece on his plate. She returned the favor by serving him some of the vegetables and then herself.

"This is delicious," he said, after taking the first bite. "It's been a long time since I've had someone cook for me."

"You probably eat out a lot?"

"No, not really. I do my own cooking, and I'm pretty good at it, too. I'll have to cook for you before you leave."

"That would be nice." She took a sip of wine.

"Tell me a little about yourself. What do you do for a living?" he asked.

"I own a bookstore in Costa Mesa. It's an artsy type community. My store is small, quaint, and has a kind of cozy feeling."

"So, you like books? What do you like to read?"

"I read everything, but mostly I like mysteries and biographies."

"We have something in common. I like mysteries, too."

"Have you read the last one that Michael Webb just released? I thought it was so good and didn't figure it out until the end."

"Don't tell me the ending. That's what I am reading now."

"I won't, but when you're finished with it, I want to hear what you thought about it."

"It's a deal. I'm almost finished, and we can talk about it over dinner at my house. How about next week?"

Karri didn't expect an invitation so fast. She was speechless for a few seconds.

"You will still be here next week, won't you?"

"Yes, I'm planning on staying for a couple weeks."

"You must have a lot of stuff to do for your aunt's estate."

"Not really, I mainly needed a vacation."

"The books getting to you?"

"Not the books, but something else." She didn't want to discuss Brent with Jake, so she directed the conversation to Kentucky.

Jake told her all about living in the commonwealth, and she found it fascinating.

"Would you like some dessert? I bought a cheesecake at the bakery in the market in town. I can make some coffee, and we can take the dessert into the living room."

"Cheesecake is my favorite. Let me clear the dishes here while you start the coffee," he offered.

They both cleared the table and took the dishes into the kitchen. While she started the coffee brewing and sliced the cheesecake, he carried in the rest of the dishes and wine. He even scraped the food off of the plates before putting them in the sink.

"Stop. Before you offer to do the dishes, let me say that I will take care of that later. You go ahead into the living room, and I'll bring in the coffee and cheesecake."

He didn't argue and went to the living room, as requested. When she walked in with the coffee and dessert, she found he had started a fire in the fireplace.

"That feels nice," she said.

"When it's cold out, a good fire always feels good." Jake came over and sat on the couch with her.

She handed him a plate with some cheesecake on it. "You told me all about Kentucky, now tell me about yourself."

He hesitated and stalled while he took a bite of his dessert and a drink of coffee. "This tastes great, and the coffee is perfect."

"As I said earlier, the cheesecake is from the store and the coffee, well the coffee's just regular store-bought. Are you avoiding my question?"

"I don't like talking about myself." He wouldn't make eye contact.

"Are you ashamed of your life, or are you hiding something?"

He took another drink of coffee, pausing again before answering. "Neither."

"Okay, let's try some simple questions. Have you always lived in Kentucky?"

"Yes."

"You really don't like talking about yourself." He almost smiled. "Do you have any family? Brothers, sisters?"

"I have a brother, Tim. No sisters and my parents are no longer living. Do you have any family?"

"Ah, ah, ah." She waved her finger at him. "This is supposed to be about you, but no I don't have any siblings. Did you go to college?"

"Yes. I went to the University of Kentucky and graduated with a degree in Business Administration and a minor in agriculture."

"Really?"

"You didn't think I went to college?"

"I didn't know. That's why I asked you." She knew she wasn't fooling him.

"Just because people are from the country doesn't mean we're stupid."

"I didn't mean to imply you were uneducated. I'm sorry if you took it that way." She felt bad she may have given him the impression he was no more than just a farmer. "Tell me about your farm."

"I own about sixty acres. I raise cattle, plant corn, and I have boarded a few horses as well as having some of my own."

"You can make a living doing just that? What do you do during the winter when the corn has been picked?"

"You ask a lot of questions."

"I'm like a sponge and want to soak up everything I can. I don't know anything about farms."

He smiled. "I sometimes work part time at the farm supply store. That way, I can get a discount on things for my farm and first shot at new products. I also have a small oil well located at the back of my land that I earn a little money from. You don't have to worry about me, I can survive all on my own," he said.

For a brief moment, she felt bad she had given him the impression she thought less of him. "Wait a minute. You intentionally made me feel bad to avoid me asking you any more questions about you. I'm right, aren't I?"

He looked over at her and flashed a smile that could melt ice, and it almost melted her. "You're good," he said. "You read people very well."

"Thank you." She was pleased with herself.

"Okay, one more question and that's your quota for this evening."

She thought for a few seconds before coming up with her question. "Why hasn't some lucky woman snapped you up?"

He hesitated before answering. "I don't know, just unlucky I guess." Jake grabbed the remote control and turned the television on scanning the channels. "Look, there's a John Wayne movie on. I love his movies. Would you like to watch that?"

"I love John Wayne, too. Let me pour you some more coffee." She freshened his cup. Karri was convinced Jake was hiding something. He had successfully found something else for them to concentrate on other than him and it just made her want to know even more. She would play along for now but had made a vow to find out what he was hiding before she left to go back to California.

By the end of the movie two hours later, Karri had made herself comfortable by slipping off her shoes and was leaning against Jake's shoulder with his arm draped around her. "That was a great movie," she said, as the credits rolled.

"It's late. I should really be going." He got up to leave.

"Late? It's only eleven o'clock."

25

"You forget, I get up with chickens," he teased.

She smiled. "Let me get your bottle of wine." She walked into the kitchen.

When she came back into the living room Jake was sitting on the edge of the couch watching the news. "They said something about snow coming tonight. I'd like to wait to hear the weather report if you wouldn't mind. I'm afraid I won't get home in time to hear it if I leave now."

"Of course, please stay. I heard something on the radio today about a chance of snow for tonight. I bet it's beautiful around here when it snows."

"If it's a light snow, it can be beautiful. But, when it's a heavy snow, we sometimes get stranded back here until the road department makes their way here to plow us out."

"Does that happen often?" She didn't like the idea of being stranded in the snow.

"Once or twice each winter is about the norm."

The meteorologist had just come on the television screen. "Tonight, it will become mostly cloudy with any flurries or snow showers ending by three a.m. The low will be near twenty-six with winds from the northwest at twenty to thirty miles per hour, diminishing to ten to fifteen miles per hour. Chance of snow is sixty percent with a slushy accumulation of less than one inch.

Tomorrow's forecast is windy with morning rain with a mix of rain and snow in the afternoon. The morning high will be around fifty degrees with temps falling to near freezing by sunset. The winds will be out of the north and gust up to thirty miles per hour. The chance of precipitation is eighty percent with snow accumulations around one inch."

Jake picked up the remote control and turned the sound down. "Well, it looks like we're in for a little snow and cold weather tonight and tomorrow."

"I am going to freeze." Her voice was slow and determined.

"It won't be that bad." He got up. "Keep the fireplace lit, curl up with a book and a cup of coffee. You'll be fine."

"You're not the one from California where it's in the eighties during the day. Trust me, I'm going to freeze."

Karri followed him as he walked to the front door.

"Dinner was great. Thank you for inviting me."

She noticed he said dinner and not supper and thought that was cute. "Here's the bottle of wine I bought for you."

He stopped at the door to put his coat on and then took the bottle from her. "Thank you. So, when do you want to have sup-- I mean dinner at my place?"

"Anytime in the next couple of weeks is fine. I don't need much notice. My calendar's pretty clear."

"I'll call you then."

"Oh, let me get you my cell phone number." She got a piece of paper out of her purse, wrote down her number and handed it to him.

"Thanks."

Both of them sort of stared at each other, not sure what to do. It was an awkward moment. Finally, Jake said, "Have a nice evening." And kissed her on the cheek before going out the door.

CHAPTER THREE

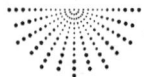

The next morning, Jake woke up feeling a warm body lying next to him, reminding him he wasn't in bed alone. He hated to move for fear of waking up his bedmate. Suddenly, he felt movement, and his companion was awake. When he felt a warm, wet tongue touch his ear he couldn't hold back any longer.

"Colt, get off of me you damn dog." Jake sat up wiping saliva from his ear with the sheet. The dog moved to the foot of the bed and sat there staring at him. "You aren't exactly my idea of who I want to wake up to every morning."

The dog laid down putting his head on the bed. Only his eyes moved, looking upward sadly at Jake.

"Get off the bed. No sympathy for you this morning. I wanted to sleep late." Jake looked out the window and saw a blanket of snow had fallen overnight. "Looks like about two inches." That meant work for him. He needed to take hay out to the cattle.

After relieving himself in the bathroom, he decided to forgo the morning shave and went to the kitchen. First, he opened the door, so Colt could go out for his morning walk. The cold air hit Jake like a brick wall. "The temperature must have dropped more than they predicted."

He turned on the small television which sat on the counter to see if he could catch any news. He ran through the channels until he found the local news but then heard someone knocking at his front door. He turned off the TV and went to the door.

The face in the window was familiar. "Tim, what are you doing here?" Jake said, letting his older brother inside.

"I wanted to see if you needed any help with the cows this morning. With the snow last night, I knew you'd have to take the hay out to them."

"I just got up and was going to fix a little breakfast before going out. If you'll eat with me, I'll let you help with the hay." Jake was teasing his brother. Both knew Jake could handle the hay himself.

"I never turn down breakfast. What's on the menu?" Tim asked following his brother back to the kitchen.

"How does bacon and eggs sound?" Jake asked while he started some coffee brewing.

"Sounds better than what Renae was fixing for breakfast when I left."

"And, what was that?" he asked while starting the bacon.

"Some kind of quiche thing with broccoli. I don't know how she expects a man to survive on that girly crap."

Jake put some bread in the four-slot toaster and pushed the lever down. He turned back to the frying bacon. "Is that why you come so often to help on the farm, so you can eat a man's breakfast?"

"You have me figured out pretty good, little brother." Tim got two cups from the cabinet and poured each of them a cup of coffee. "By the time I get the hay out to the first pasture, I'm starved."

Both men laughed. Jake heard scratching at the door and opened it to let Colt back in and poured some dog food in a bowl for him. The toast popped up and Jake buttered each slice placing them on the plates and turning his attention to the eggs now frying in the skillet. "Doesn't she realize you need more food?"

"She says she looking out for my health. I need red meat for my health." Again, both men laughed and soon they were sitting at the table eating their breakfast.

"What's this?" Tim picked up the bottle of wine that Karri had given to Jake the night before.

"A gift."

"From who?" Tim prodded.

Jake hated to answer but knew his brother would keep at him until he knew all about the previous night with Karri.

"Alma Carter's great-niece is staying back at her house while she gets things settled with the estate. I met her yesterday and she asked me over for supper last night. She gave the wine to me."

"Whoa." Tim stopped holding the fork of egg in the air in front of him. "Is there something you're not telling me? What did you do to deserve a bottle of wine?"

"Nothing like that. She arrived very late Thursday night. I knew there was nothing in that house to eat, so Friday morning I took some biscuits and sorghum to her for breakfast. She repaid me by asking me for supper."

"That's great. It's about time you started seeing someone again," Tim said, swallowed the eggs from the fork.

"I'm not seeing her. She's only here for a few weeks and then she goes back to California. It was just the neighborly thing to do, okay."

"Well, maybe the neighborly thing to do would be for Renae and I to have you two over for supper one night this week," Tim teased.

Finished with his meal, Jake got up to put his plate in the sink. "Don't bother. Like I said, it's not like that. Now, do you want to help feed the cattle, or not?"

"Let's go," Tim answered.

The men grabbed their coats and headed out the door, with the dog following. As they walked toward the barn, Jake could hear a car engine running from the direction of Karri's aunt's house. He stood still listening.

"What's wrong?" Tim asked.

"Listen. Do you hear that motor running?"

"Yeah, it sounds like someone's stuck."

"Crazy city woman. I bet she's trying to drive her car out in this snow."

"Don't you think we should go help her out? After all, it's the neighborly thing to do," Tim said, teasing him again.

Jake shook his head in defeat. "Let's go help her."

"Great. We'll take my truck. It's already warmed up," Tim said.

The men got into Tim's truck and Colt jumped into the back for the short drive back to Karri's.

When they arrived, they saw Karri in the car with its back wheels buried in the snow and the mud. She turned the engine off and got out of the car. Jake tried to hide his laughter. She was dressed in tight blue jeans that were tucked into knee-high boots with a spiked heel. She wore no coat, but only a lightweight sweater and a scarf circled her neck. Her hands and lips looked white from the cold.

"Need some help?" Jake asked.

"I sure do. I don't know how I got it stuck."

"The ground isn't frozen under the snow yet. You backed the car into some mud and the tires couldn't get any traction. To tell you the truth, you really have no business driving in this snow without knowing what you're doing."

"I need to go shopping. With this cold weather hitting, I didn't bring enough warm clothes." She looked over at Tim.

"This is my brother, Tim Duncan. He lives down the road from here with his wife and son. Tim, this is Karri Taylor, Alma's great-niece."

"Pleasure, ma'am." He extended his hand to her.

"The pleasure is all mine," she said, shaking his hand.

"You better get some gloves on. Your hand feels like ice," Tim said.

"That's on my shopping list, but it doesn't look like I'm going to be going anywhere today."

"We can have that car out in no time, but Jake is right about you not driving. If you don't know how to drive in snow, you really shouldn't be out," Tim said. "The highway department hasn't had time to salt all the roads yet."

"I know, but I really need to do a little shopping. If you can get the car out, I promise to be careful and drive slowly," Karri said.

Jake thought for a moment before speaking. "We'll pull your car out, but I'll drive you to do your shopping."

"I couldn't let you do that. It would be too much of an imposition."

"You are not imposing at all. Besides, I need to pick up a few things in town anyway." He looked over at Tim, who was grinning from ear-to-ear. He knew he would never hear the end of this.

"I've got a tow strap in the truck." Tim said. He was already opening the lid of the toolbox that was attached to the bed.

"I really appreciate you doing this. I hate being such a problem," Karri said.

"You're not a problem. Around here, neighbors help each other. After we get your car out, I'll need to go change clothes before we leave for town."

"Okay. I could wait at your house, if you don't mind, so you won't have to drive back here again to get me."

Jake nodded. Tim had moved the truck in front of the car and had attached the tow strap to the bumper of Karri's rental car. Tim got in the truck and Jake got in the car and started the engine. When he signaled Tim that he was ready, both men put their vehicles into gear.

The tow strap stretched taunt as the gears of the truck began to grind. Karri thought the strap might break and moved several feet back. Jake's dog walked over and stood behind her.

Both vehicles began to move slightly, and after several attempts, the back wheels of the car finally rolled out of the hole it was buried in.

Jake parked the car in front of the house, got out and handed her the keys. "That wasn't too bad, and I don't think there was any damage to the car."

"That's good. I just need to get my purse and I can ride to the house with you."

"Sure."

Tim removed the tow strap from the vehicles and stowed it back in the toolbox. Jake noticed the smile Tim was trying to hide while listening to their conversation. He was a little worried at what Tim would tell Karri while he was changing clothes. His life and his past were something he wasn't ready to share with someone he had just met.

She was back next to them in no time.

"Come on, Karri. You can sit between us in the truck," Tim said.

Karri climbed into the four-wheel drive and positioned herself between the two men for the short drive up the road to Jake's house. Colt jumped in the back again.

"Jake tells me you're from California. How long are you going to be visiting here?" Tim asked.

"Only for a couple weeks to finish up some business with my great-aunt's estate."

"Well, before you leave, you will have to come and have supper with my wife and myself. You can join us too, right Jake?"

Jake mumbled in agreement, but he wasn't happy about it. He knew his brother was working on getting he and Karri together, but it wasn't going to work. She wouldn't be here long enough for a relationship, and that was fine with him. He had no intention of getting involved with anyone again, at least not for a long time.

Back at Jake's house, the three of them got out and walked into the home, with the dog following in their tracks.

"It won't take me a minute to get ready," Jake said. He wanted to be as quick as possible so Tim wouldn't have as much time to talk to Karri alone. While he went to the bedroom to change, Tim and Karri stepped into the living room to wait. As soon as they sat down, the telephone rang.

"I'll get it," Tim called to Jake, as he picked up the phone on the table next to the couch. "Hello."

While Tim was on the phone, Karri decided to look around the cabin. The living room was large with a chair on each side of the couch and tables in between. A huge fireplace was in the middle of the wall across from the couch with stone tiles in front of the fireplace. The room also featured a wood stove with the stovepipe exiting through the wall near the roof, and a bay window which offered a view of the driveway.

The hallway that Jake had gone into must lead to the bedrooms.

The doorway on the opposite side was the entry into the kitchen and Karri could see a small dining table next to a window looking out onto the woods behind the cabin. She'd never seen so many cabinets in a kitchen. On the other side of the kitchen was a doorway that led to what looked like a utility room with a door leading outside.

The cabin had a very cozy feel to it. She walked over to the fireplace to glance at the framed photos. One picture on the mantle caught her attention. It was a photo of Jake with a woman, and they were posed like a couple. Another photo was of the two of them with his dog.

Tim finished his call and hung up the phone and Karri turned toward him.

"My wife needs me at home. It was very nice meeting you, Karri and I meant what I said about coming for supper before you leave." He started to the door.

"I'd love to meet your wife. Jake has my phone number, just give me a call and let me know when to be there."

"Great. Tell Jake I had to get home and I was sorry for not helping with the cattle."

"I will."

Tim walked out the front door before Karri had the chance to ask about the photo of Jake and the woman.

A few minutes later, Jake came out of the bedroom and looked around. "Where's Tim?"

"His wife called and he had to leave. He said something about being sorry he couldn't help with the cattle," Karri said.

"I guess I'm ready if you are."

"If you need to take care of your cows, I can go to town myself."

"No, it's fine. I need to feed the cattle, but it can wait until I get back. My barn manager should be here soon and he'll take care of it."

"I need to use the restroom first."

"Down the hall."

When Karri came back out, she was very talkative. "You have a beautiful cabin and I love your bathroom. Did you install that bathtub inside all that creek stone yourself?"

34

"No, that came with the place." He grabbed his keys from the peg by the door and opened it for her. They stepped out into the sunshine, albeit a cold sunshine.

"So, you bought this house then?"

Jake didn't want to get into details about the house. "No."

Unusual answer, she thought.

After Colt came outside, Jake locked the door and they got into his truck. "Tell me again what you're going shopping for so I'll know where to take you."

"I need some warmer clothes, shoes, and a few more groceries."

"Sounds like a Wal-Mart trip to me." Jake started the truck and drove down the driveway.

"Wal-Mart?"

"You do have Wal-Mart's in California, don't you?"

"Yes, but I was thinking of stores like Nordstrom's or Alexander's."

"Stores like that would be over an hour drive. Wal-Mart is only about thirty minutes from here. You can find the kind of clothes you need there."

"What do you mean the kind of clothes I need? What kind of clothes do you think I need?"

Wrong thing to say, he thought to himself. "If you want warm clothes, you need to get practical clothes, not that designer stuff."

"What's wrong with my designer clothes?"

"There's nothing wrong with them. I think you look great in them, but apparently, they don't keep you warm. And, you'll break an ankle walking in the snow with those spiked heels. You need a good pair of snow boots."

She was quiet for a moment. "I suppose you're right."

Jake felt as though she was angry with him. "I'm sorry if I offended you. Your clothes are fine to wear around here. I just don't think you should wear them in this type of weather." He was probably digging himself deeper but wanted to explain what he had meant. "Besides, Wal-Mart is like one-stop shopping. They will have everything we need to get today."

"We? So, this trip isn't just for me. You're shopping too?"

"If I'm cooking supper for you tonight, I need to buy the main course."

"I'm invited to dinner?"

"Yes. Didn't I mention that earlier?"

"No, I don't believe you did and what are you preparing?"

"It's a secret; a very special recipe." He wasn't panicking yet, but if he couldn't make a decision on a menu during the drive to the store, he would be in big trouble.

"The countryside is beautiful out here with all this snow," Karri said.

No one else had ventured out yet, and as the truck moved slowly over the road, it christened the virgin snow which had fallen the night before.

"That's what I love about living here. I never get tired of the sight of a snow-covered pasture. One of my favorite things to do is to take a walk in the woods after a snowfall. It's so peaceful, and all you can hear are your footsteps crunching in the snow."

"Sounds wonderful. Maybe I'll do just that after we return from the store today."

"You shouldn't go into the woods alone. It's too dangerous."

"Don't worry, I won't get lost."

"That's not what I meant. In the wintertime, and especially with snow on the ground, the coyotes will be out looking for food. A couple of the farmers have seen one acting strangely and we are worried about rabies. They can be aggressive and come after you instead when they are infected." They had reached the highway and turned east toward the town where the Wal-Mart was located.

"Really? I had no idea. But, you go walking in the woods."

"I'm experienced, and I never go out in the woods without a gun for protection."

"I see. There's a lot to learn about living in the country."

"If you want, you can come with me when I go out to feed the cattle later. I'll be using the tractor to take some hay out to the back pasture."

"On a tractor? Where would I sit?"

Jake laughed. "The tractor I have has a heated cabin and room for two."

"Heated. I didn't know they made heated tractors."

"You do have a lot to learn about living on a farm."

"I won't be here long enough to worry about that and I'd love to see you in Los Angeles. You'd probably say 'howdy' to someone on the street and they'd shoot you."

"You're probably right. I'm not sure I could survive in a city. I'm not sure I would want to," Jake said.

"What's wrong with living in a city?"

"There's nothing wrong with it if that's what you want. I like living in the country with the open spaces, clean air, no noise, and a clear sky at night to see the stars."

"There are advantages to living in a big city, too. For instance, I don't have to drive thirty minutes to get to a store to buy groceries."

"Okay, point taken. This trip would not be as far if we were in the city."

"Not only that, this trip would not be necessary in my hometown because it doesn't snow there. I also can go out at almost any time at night and find a market open to pick up milk, bread or eggs."

He had her now. "I can get eggs any time I need them, too. I just walk out to the chicken coop and gather the one's the chickens laid the night before."

She smiled at that remark.

"Don't you think you'd like living here? How could someone not like how beautiful it is around here when it snows?" he asked.

"I can drive about two hours to Bear Mountain and see all the snow I want and have a great day of skiing. Can you spend the day skiing around here?"

"As a matter of fact, I can. If I wanted to, that is."

He glanced over toward her and noticed a shocked look on her face. He could see her trying to figure out how he could ski in Kentucky.

"Okay, I give up. Skiing around here? How do you do that, or are you talking about cross-country skiing?"

"Nope, not cross-country. There's a ski area in the next county north of here. They don't have big mountains like I'm sure you have out in California, but there are some pretty good hills. Enough to keep the locals entertained and challenged."

"Do you ski?"

"Not me. I've been up by the place but never had enough nerve to give it a try. Tim and his wife have gone there a few times though. I'm guessing you ski?"

"Yes, I love to ski."

Jake turned the truck right at the stoplight and into the parking lot.

"Is there a Starbucks around here? I'd love some coffee."

"No, we don't have any place like that. If you want, we could go through McDonald's drive-thru window for coffee."

"No, that's okay. I really wanted some Starbuck's. That's how I always start my days back home. A stop at their coffee shop is routine for me on the way to work. I'll just see if they have some of their coffee grounds in the store."

After finding a place to park, they got out and went into the store. It was crowded for so early in the day. Karri headed for the ladies' clothes and Jake reluctantly followed. He wasn't sure he should help her shop for clothes.

"Karri, why don't we split up? You do your shopping, and I'll go get the groceries I need for tonight."

"Okay. That sounds like a good idea. We can probably finish faster that way. How about we meet at the snack bar by the door we came through in about an hour?"

An hour, he thought. He'd be finished in twenty minutes, counting the time at the checkout. "I'll see you in an hour."

Jake headed to the produce department to get some salad ingredients. Next, he went to find the main course. He wanted to impress her and prove he wasn't just any old country boy and could prepare a meal fit for a queen. Wandering the isles, it came to him what he would fix for her. After stops in the pasta and dairy section and the bakery, he was almost ready to go to the checkout. He had one more stop to make to get something special for Karri. Finally, after paying for his items, he sat in at the snack bar to wait for her.

Thirty minutes later, he saw Karri walking toward him with a cart full of bags. He got up to meet her.

"Are you ready to go?" he asked.

"Can we get something to eat before we go back?"

"Sure, what kind of food do you want?"

"I don't know what kind of places you have around here. You chose," she said.

"There's a little restaurant downtown that is pretty good if you'd like to go there."

"Sounds great."

They loaded their bags in the backseat of the truck and Jake drove them down to the town square. After parking, they walked to the Copper Creek Cafe and entered the restaurant through their gift shop. Karri took her time looking at the gift baskets, coffee mixes, seasonal decorations, and confections.

At the doorway to the restaurant, Jake asked the hostess for a table for two and she led them to one in the corner. Jake held the chair for Karri and then took his seat. Both of them ordered coffee to drink and looked over the menu while waiting for their drinks.

"What's good here?" Karri asked.

"I haven't eaten here in a while, but best I remember their soup in a bread bowl is their specialty."

"The blackboard where we came in said the soup of the day is cheddar broccoli. That's my favorite. I'll have to try that." She closed the menu and placed it on the table next to her.

Jake was still undecided when the waitress came back with their coffee and two glasses of ice water.

"Are you ready to order, or do you need more time?" she asked.

Jake looked at Karri. "Go ahead and order."

"I'll have your soup of the day in a bread bowl," she said.

"And, I'll take a Club Sandwich with fries."

"Thank you." The waitress took their menus and left with the orders.

After they got their food and finished eating, they left the restaurant and with the sidewalk cleared of snow, they took a little walk around town before heading back to Jake's truck. The town square across the street looked beautiful with all the winter decorations that had been put into place.

"I love all the little shops and antique stores in this town. After the roads are cleared, I want to drive back and buy some things to ship home."

"You can find some good bargains here, if you're willing to look hard enough," Jake said, as they continued around the square. "Here's my truck, we'd better get back and put these groceries away."

He opened the door for her and she stepped up into the truck. The drive home was full of conversation, mostly hers. She talked about all the things she saw in the windows of the shops that she wanted to buy. When they turned back onto the gravel road that led to their homes, she noticed the snow had been plowed off and driving seemed much easier than it was when they had left earlier.

"The highway department sure is good around here. They even plowed the driveway back to Aunt Alma's house," Karri noted.

"They didn't do that. I suspect Tim got his tractor out and did that for you."

"That was very nice of him. I'll have to make sure and thank him."

Jake pulled the truck to a stop in front of her house and turned off the engine.

"I'll help you carry your things in," he said.

"Thanks." She grabbed a bag and went to unlock the door. She came back out just as he was entering the house and ran right into him nearly knocking the bags out of his hands. "I'm sorry. I should have looked before I came out."

"No, it was my fault. I knew you would be coming back out." Both of them started laughing at their silliness.

"This is the last of your bags," he said.

She took the small bag of clothes from him. "Thanks."

"Don't forget to come for dinner tonight around six, okay?"

"I'll be there. I can't wait to see if you're the cook you claim to be."

Jake liked the way she smiled when she said that. It had been a long time since he enjoyed a woman's smile and he was really enjoying this one. He waved goodbye to her and got in his truck to leave. His thoughts now went to fixing the dinner for her tonight and a little prayer that it wouldn't ruin it.

CHAPTER FOUR

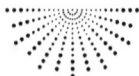

"First, I got the car stuck the snow and mud in the driveway, and he had to pull it out and then he took me shopping so I could get some warmer clothes." As Karri talked over the phone with Alex, she walked into the kitchen to pour herself another cup of coffee.

"Karri, you have got to e-mail me a photo of this guy. He sounds like a knight in shining armor," Alex said.

"Oh, and there are no Starbucks around here. I couldn't even find any bags of their coffee grounds at the store. I'm going through withdrawal and have to settle for regular coffee."

"Do you want me to FedEx you some?"

"No, I'm so far out in the middle of nowhere, it would probably take forever for a delivery person to find me. I'll just have to make do with what I have until I get home. But I can promise you, the first thing I will do after I get off the plane is get some of that coffee." Back in the living room, she sat down on the couch and put her feet up.

"Tell me more about Jake. What does he look like?" Alex asked.

"Well, I have to admit, he's gorgeous. He's in his 30's, tall, has broad shoulders, brown hair, and brown eyes. I don't know if he works out, or if it's all the work he does on his farm, but that man has a set of muscles you wouldn't believe."

"Sounds like you have found a replacement for Brent."

"Replacement? No, not likely. This guy's a farmer, what kind of future does a farmer have? You know the men I like are well educated and financially sound. All you hear about farmers is how they are all on the verge of losing their farms to the bank or about to get gobbled up by some big company wanting to take over."

"Well, don't count your chickens before they're hatched."

Karri laughed. "Alex, you would fit right in here. Anyway, I am going to his house for dinner tonight, and he's cooking. He said he wants to repay me for the dinner I prepared for him."

"If you ask me, it sounds like he's got his eyes set on you."

"I'm not asking you and he's just being neighborly."

"If you say so. Call me again tomorrow, okay? I want to hear every detail and don't forget to take a picture of him with your phone and send it to me," Alex said.

"Oh, I'm not sure how I could take a picture of him without him knowing and I don't think I could tell him why I was doing it if he caught me."

"Do the best you can."

"I'll see. What are you doing tonight?"

"I'm meeting Andy for drinks at the Scoreboard Bar."

"You're going out with Brent's brother?"

"I'm sorry, Karri. I know he's Brent's brother, but we ran into each other a few nights ago and really hit it off."

"Just be careful. Hopefully, he's not the jerk Brent is."

"I will. You have fun tonight."

"Okay. Bye." Karri hung up her cell phone and finished her coffee.

The day went by fast. She'd been so busy sorting through Alma's things to donate, she'd lost track of time. After she finished filling another bag with clothes, she went to get ready for dinner with Jake.

In the bathroom, she filled the tub with hot water, adding a few drops of scented bath oil she'd purchased earlier in the day. After pulling her hair up, she stepped into the tub and let the hot water relax her while she thought about how the night would go. Dinner with Jake had to be different than dinner with Brent. She never got to make her own choices. He always ordered their food, drinks, and even chose the restaurant. Jake would be different; she could feel it.

She had just finished her bath and dried off when her cell phone rang. "Hello."

"Karri, it's Jake Duncan. I'm so sorry, but I'm going to have to cancel our dinner tonight."

"Oh, that's too bad. Is something wrong?"

"I have an emergency with one of my horses, and I need to tend to her."

"What happened?"

"I'm not sure. My barn manager just called and said he found her down in her stall. I've called the vet and he's on the way."

"I'm so sorry. Is there anything I can do?"

"It's not as nice as dinner, but you can come to the barn with me if you want. Most of my workers have already gone home and we might need an extra hand."

"I don't know how much help I can be, but I'll do what I can."

"I'll be back to pick you up in a few minutes. Dress in warm clothes. It can get kind of cold in the barn."

"I'll be ready." She hung up the phone and started grabbing the clothes she'd just bought that day. Sweater, jeans, heavy socks, boots, a new coat, scarf, and finally a pair of gloves. She rushed out when she heard his truck pull up and climbed inside. "Hi." The first thing she noticed was the worried look on his face.

"Hi." He put the truck in gear and sped back toward his house and then to the horse barn beyond. "I'm sorry about dinner, but it's nice of you to come help."

"Like I said on the phone, I don't know how much help I can be, but I'll be there for moral support." She looked in the backseat of the truck where Colt was laying with his head down. Even he looked worried if that were possible for a dog.

As they neared the barn, Karri saw a pickup truck and an SUV parked by the door.

"Looks like Doc Jordan is already here," Jake said. He parked next to the SUV, and they entered the barn.

Karri followed Jake to a room that was a combination kitchen and office with two men standing inside.

"Doc, thanks for coming out," Jake said, as he shook the older man's hand. "This is Karri Taylor, Alma Carter's great-niece. Karri, this is Doc Jordan, and this is Marty Johnson, my barn manager."

"Miss Taylor, your Aunt Alma was a dear friend to my wife and I. She is certainly missed around here," Doc Jordan said.

"She sure is," Marty added. "Especially those chocolate chip cookies she used to bring to the church picnics."

"Thank you. It's nice hearing about her from everyone here. I'm afraid I don't remember much about her since I was really young the last time I visited."

"Doc, how's Chestnut?" Jake asked with a serious tone.

"I think she has colic."

Jake let out an exasperated breath. Karri followed Jake and Doc out of the office and back to one of the stalls where a beautiful chestnut-colored horse laid in the straw. Colt already sat at the stall door as if on guard.

Karri knew nothing about horse ailments, but from the look on everyone's face, she could tell it was serious.

Doc went into the stall first, then Jake and Marty. She stood next to Colt and scratched his ears while listening to the men talk.

"I took some fluid samples from her, but from the way her intestines sound and how she acts, I'm pretty sure it's colic. I gave her an injection to help with her pain and I'll send the samples to the equine lab at the University of Kentucky, but I really think we should start treating her now instead of waiting."

"I think you're right. Do whatever you need," Jake said. He stepped out of the stall and stood next to Karri.

"Colic is serious, right?" she asked.

"It's the number one killer of horses."

Marty stepped out to join them. "I think it was the hay, boss."

"Why do you think that?"

"We just got that new shipment delivered earlier this week. Yesterday is when I started feeding it to the horses. I found mold growing on one of the bales. You know that can cause colic."

"Have any of the other horses eaten from that shipment?" Jake asked.

"Probably. I'll have to ask the workers in the morning to be sure."

"Can you call them tonight to find out? If they did, I want Doc to check them too."

"I'll do that." Marty walked back to the office.

Doc finished with Chestnut and stepped out of the stall.

"Marty found a molded bale of hay Chestnut may have eaten. Some of the other horses may have too. Could you check on them before you go?"

"Yes. I better do that. If we can catch this early, it could make a difference with the other horses." He left to do his examinations.

Karri heard the barn door open and both she and Jake looked that direction. Tim walked in and held the door open for a little boy followed by a woman.

"Uncle Jake!" The boy ran up to Jake and jumped into his arms. "Daddy said Chestnut is sick. Is she gonna be okay? I brought her a sugar cube." The little boy held out his damp hand that held a partially dissolved sugar cube.

Tim and the woman walked up. "Brian wouldn't go to bed until we brought him down here to see if Chestnut was okay," Tim said.

Jake looked at Brian. "Doc Jordan gave her some medicine, so we'll just have to wait and see how she does. She can't have the sugar right now, but why don't you put it by her feed bag so she'll find it when she feels like eating."

Jake put the boy down, and he did as Jake said.

"I brought some sandwiches and potato salad," the woman said, lifting a basket. "I figured you'd have a long night."

"Thanks, Renae. Oh, this is Karri Taylor, Alma's great-niece. Karri, this is Tim's wife, Renae."

"I did it." Brian came running back to the group.

"And, this little fella is their son, Brian."

"Hi. Are you Uncle Jake's girlfriend?"

Tim tried to hold in a laugh and Jake was speechless.

Karri looked down at Brian. "I'm just a friend visiting from California."

"Oh, okay." Brian then ran to pet Colt.

"I'm going to put these sandwiches in the refrigerator in the office. Brian, come with me. You need to wash your hands. Should I make a pot of coffee?" Renae asked.

"We could sure use some. Thanks, Renae," Jake said.

"I'll help you," Karri said.

The ladies walked to the office.

"You said you're from California. I bet you've never spent the night in a barn caring for a four-legged animal before."

"No, but I've cared for a two-legged one I'd like to have taken a cattle prod to." Karri took the coffee pot and filled it with water.

"Most women around here have wanted to do that at one time or another. The coffee is in that cabinet above the coffee maker." Renae put the sandwiches and potato salad in the refrigerator.

"Mommy, I washed my hands. Can I go back out?" Brian asked.

"Let me see." He held up his hands for inspection. "Okay, you're good. Get going." She turned back to Karri. "How do you like it here in the country?"

"I've only been here for a few days. It's definitely different than home, but so far I like it." After setting the coffee maker up, Karri pushed the button to start the brewing. "Jake really cares about his animals, doesn't he?"

"He really does, but especially that horse."

"What's so special about this horse?"

"She was his wife's horse."

Karri sat down, puzzled.

"He didn't tell you about his wife?"

"I saw a photo of him with a woman at his house, but I didn't know who she was."

"Her name was Loren."

"Was?"

"She was killed in an auto accident about a year ago. She was driving home at night during a snowstorm. She skidded on some ice and hit a tree. She had taken a different route home and wasn't found for hours. Jake was devastated. Honestly, until you came around, he's not shown any interest in a woman since."

"Me? Oh, you have that wrong. He's just being nice. There's not anything going on between us. I'll be going back home in a few weeks anyway."

"What do you do back home?" Renae grabbed a bag of cookies out of the basket, took one of them and then offered some to Karri.

"I own a bookstore in Costa Mesa." She picked one of the cookies and took a bite.

"Costa Mesa? That's an artist community, isn't it?" She got up to get some coffee cups out of the cabinet.

"Yes. Have you been there?"

"No, but I teach art at the high school, so I've heard of it."

"You teach art? After tasting these cookies, I would have guessed you taught home-ec. They're delicious."

"They're my favorite too." Jake walked in and snatched a couple from the bag. Tim, right behind him, did the same. "Doc Jordan just left. He checked the other horses and said they look okay, but we need to watch them closely."

"Where's Brian?" Renae asked.

"We left him with Chestnut," Tim replied.

"You left him with a sick horse?" René turned and started out of the kitchen with Tim following after her.

"How long before you'll know if Chestnut will be okay?" Karri asked.

"I don't know. It could be in the morning, or it could be in a couple of days. I'm going to stay and watch over her tonight. Tim said he and Renae will take you back to your house."

"That's nice of them, but I'd love to stay here tonight too, if that's okay? I could never experience anything like this back home, and besides, you need someone to keep you company."

"You want to spend the night in a cold barn with the horses?"

"And, with you too. Yes."

"Well, okay. I think we have some extra blankets in a closet somewhere."

Karri followed Jake out into the barn and saw Tim and Renae searching the stalls. "What are you looking for?" Jake asked.

"Brian disappeared again," Tim replied.

"Oh, my gosh." Karri joined in the search with Renae. "You don't seem to scared."

"This isn't the first time he's wandered off. He never goes very far. He's in the barn somewhere."

"Found him," Tim called from the back stall.

Everyone rushed back to find Brian sleeping in the hay with Colt next to him. Tim picked him up and walked out with Brian slumped over his shoulder. "We're going to head home. Karri, we'd be glad to drop you off," he said.

"I'm going to stay here tonight and help Jake watch over the horses, but thanks for offering."

"Really?" Renae smiled. "When you get hungry, the rest of the food is in the refrigerator." She tried to sneak a wink at Jake, but Karri caught it.

"Thanks for bringing it," Jake said. "I'll talk to you tomorrow."

The family left as Marty walked in. "Did I hear someone say food?"

"Renae left some stuff in the fridge."

"Let me get everything out and we can all sit down and eat," Karri offered and they went to the kitchen.

Marty fixed himself a plate and went back out to watch over Chestnut while Jake and Karri sat down at the table to eat.

"She's a beautiful horse, Jake. I can tell you care about her."

"She's one of my favorites. I hate seeing any of my animals sick, but Chestnut, she's special."

"René told me she was your wife's horse."

"She told you?"

"Yes, and about her accident. I'm so sorry." She reached across and touched his hand.

He didn't pull back, but instead took her hand into his. "It's taken me a long time to get over her being gone. It's been nice getting to know you this week. I think meeting someone new has helped me."

Karri smiled. "It's helped me too. I just got out of a relationship. I could have handled Alma's estate through the mail, but I needed to get away, and a trip to Kentucky seemed right. I 'm glad I came."

"It would be nice if you could stay for a while longer."

"I don't know." She felt a little uncomfortable. "I needed to get away, but I'll need to get back to my store."

Jake let go of her hand. "I should probably tell Marty you're going to stay and help." He stood. "The only place to sleep in here are in the stalls on the straw."

"That's fine with me. I just want to clean up in here and put the food away."

"I'll get the blankets." He walked out of the room.

Later in the night, Karri sat on top of the straw with a blanket over her next to Chestnut. Colt had joined her in the vigil over the horse.

Jake stepped into the stall carrying his blanket. "There's a clean stall over there where you can have more room to sleep."

"Where are you going to sleep?"

"I'm going to stay in here with the horse."

"Can I stay in here with you?"

"You want to sleep in here?"

"I want to help watch over her." She gestured toward the horse.

"If you want." He handed her a couple of blankets. "It'll get colder tonight. We have that heater over there running, but it can't keep the barn as warm as a house."

"Where's Marty going to sleep?"

"He's in a stall in the back where we found Brian earlier."

Karri took the blankets and draped them over her. Jake sat down next to her doing the same with his blankets.

Very early the next morning, something woke Karri from her sleep. She looked next to her and saw Jake still asleep. Kentucky was such a different place than her home in California. She would never have thought in the few days she'd been here, that she felt so at home. Jake and his extended family had welcomed her like one of her own. She was sure most of that was due to her late aunt.

She looked over at him again. He was like no one she'd ever met before. Such the southern gentleman, yet when it mattered, he took control. She saw the care and concern he had for his animals and wondered if he was as gentle with his women as he was with his horses.

Suddenly, Karri realized what had awoken her. Chestnut was beginning to stir. "Jake, wake up."

His eyes shot open and he sat right up. He looked quite the sight with straw sticking out of his hair.

"Chestnut's moving around."

Jake jumped up, as did Karri. "Would you go get Marty? We need to get her up and outside," he said.

Karri did as he instructed and when she and Marty got back to the stall, Jake was trying to get the horse to stand.

"Karri, would you hold onto the cheek piece of her bridle while Marty and I try to get her up?"

Karri walked around the horse and hesitated before she grabbed the leather strap at the side of her head. "Come on, girl. You have to get up and walk around. Don't let this beat you. If you get up, I promise to give you a good brushing and a bright red apple when it's allowed." She gave the horse a little rub on her nose and up she sprang.

"Well, I'll be damned. Did you see that, boss?" Marty asked.

"I sure did. Come on, we need to get her outside before it's too late." Jake spoke too soon because just as he moved behind Chestnut, she defecated all over him.

Marty broke into laughter and Karri tried her best not to, but was failing miserably.

"Hey boss, I think Chestnut's going to be okay now," Marty said.

"You think? Take her outside, please."

Marty took the horse from Karri and led her outside.

Karri and Jake both looked at each other and then broke into laughter.

"I'm sorry about this," he said.

"I'm not. Do you know how funny this is going to be when I tell my friend Alex? She's going to die laughing. Wait. Don't move. Let me get a picture." She took out her cell phone and Jake posed for the picture. "Will Chestnut be okay now," Karri asked.

"I think so. Marty will walk her around outside so she can empty her bowels and Doc will be by first thing in the morning to check on her."

"That's good. Don't you think you should get out of those stinky clothes?" She waved her hand in front of her nose.

"What? You don't like how I smell?" He took a step toward her with a devilish grin on his face.

"Don't you dare touch me with that horse crap on you." She took a couple steps back, but was cornered.

With Jake's next step, Colt ran between them and barked at him.

"What the heck? I thought you were my dog, not hers."

"He's protecting me. Good dog, Colt," she said.

"I guess so. Traitor," Jake said to the dog. "I need to clean the stall before I clean myself. Why don't you go out and check on Chestnut while I do that?" He reached up and picked a piece of straw from her hair.

"I'll wait outside then." She smiled and left the barn.

About an hour later, the sun was rising and Karri saw Jake walking toward them. Marty had put Chestnut into a corral, and Doc Jordan had already arrived and just finished checking on her.

"How is she doing, Doc?" Jake asked. He looked a little cleaner than he did earlier.

"I believe she'll be fine. I understand she voided her bowels pretty good." Doc couldn't control his chuckle and neither could Karri.

"All right, very funny. It's not the first time I've had horse shit on me and it won't be the last."

"I'll admit, I've had my share also," Doc said. "I just gave her another shot of antibiotics. Keep her moving around today and away from that hay and I think she'll make a full recovery. She'll also need plenty of water to drink."

"Thanks, Doc. You don't know how much I appreciate what you did."

"Well, that's what I'm here for. Make sure you get that hay tested."

"I'm going to take a sample to the university today," Jake said.

"Let me know what they say. I have other farms to visit, so I need to get going. It was nice meeting you last night, Miss Taylor. I hope we will meet again."

"I hope so too," she replied.

The doctor got into his truck and left.

"I suppose I need to get you back home," Jake said.

"It was a long night." They both walked to Jake's truck and he opened the door for her.

They started the drive back to Karri's house. "What will happen if the hay caused the colic?"

"The first thing I'll do is have a big bonfire to burn the rest of that hay. Then, I'll contact the farm we got the hay from and inform them of the problem. Hopefully, they will give me a full refund."

"And, if they don't?"

"Then, we have a problem. That hay cost a lot and I'll have to replace it. If they don't make good on it, I'll have to call my lawyer."

"I've never really thought about everything involved in running a farm. It's both fascinating and expensive."

Jake stopped the truck in front of her house and Karri opened her door to get out.

"Would you like to come in for some breakfast or coffee?" she asked.

"I think I better get home and get cleaned up."

"You have to eat."

"I'll grab some of the leftovers from last night. I want to get on the road to the university with that hay sample."

"Of course, I forgot." She started to close the door.

"You know, I still owe you that dinner."

"You don't have to do that."

"Are you kidding? After helping with Chestnut, I owe you even more now."

She smiled. "It was actually kind of fun."

"I'll call you when I get back from the university. Get some sleep."

"I will."

Jake put his truck in gear and drove away.

CHAPTER FIVE

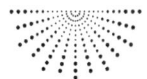

"You mean you have someone interested in buying my aunt's farm so soon, Mr. Gilmore?" Karri sat across the desk from her aunt's attorney.

"Yes, ma'am. They've offered a good price, more than market value, for the farm."

"Who would pay more than market value for it?"

"I'm not sure who it is. I've been dealing through a real estate agency out of Lexington, and they won't reveal the name of the buyer."

She paused. "Don't you think it's a little odd that someone would offer more than the property is worth?"

"I suppose they want it pretty bad. Should I draw up the purchase agreement?" he asked in his thick southern accent.

"I'd like to think about it for a few days."

"What? I thought you'd jump at the chance to sell."

Karri rose to leave. "I do want to sell it, but that farm is a special place, and I want to be certain that it's going to the right person."

Gilmore stood and rushed to the door ahead of her, grabbing the doorknob. "Ma'am, when I first met with you, I was under the impression you wanted to sell as soon as possible. Why the change?"

"I just don't think my Aunt Alma would want to sell so fast. See if you can persuade that real estate agent to tell you who the buyer is." She reached over and touched his arm. "If you find out, I might just reconsider. Now, if you'll excuse me, I have a few stops to make before going back to the farm." She withdrew her hand and waited for him to open the door.

"But, Miss Taylor, do I tell them you'll accept their offer?"

Karri looked at Gilmore's hand still on the knob of the unopened door and then looked up at him. "I'll think about it."

He finally opened the door and Karri walked out. Later that afternoon, she was just finishing the laundry when her cell phone rang. "Hello."

"Hi Kerri, it's Jake. I'm on my way back from the university and wanted to tell you what they discovered with the hay."

"You have the results already?"

"One of the guys who works in the lab is a college buddy of mine and he rushed it through as a favor."

"What did they find out?"

"The hay had milkweed in it."

"Milkweed?"

"If eaten by a horse, it can cause colic and even death. It was all through the hay."

"What will you do now?" she asked.

"I'm going to pick up Tim and then we're going over to the farm where I bought the hay and see what they say about it. If they'll give me a refund, everything will be okay. If not, then I'll have a problem."

"Make sure and keep me updated. Oh, I was at Mr. Gilmore's office this morning, and someone made an offer on Aunt Alma's farm. It was more than market value. Can you believe that?"

"You didn't accept it, did you?"

"What? No, not yet. Why?" She was confused by his concern.

"I'm going to lose my phone signal here in a minute. Can you come to my house for dinner tonight around seven? We can talk then."

"Seven? Yes, I'll be there. Do you want me to bring anything?"

There was no answer. He must have lost the signal like he said, she thought.

When she drove up to Jake's house at seven o'clock, there was a car parked in front she didn't recognize. She got out, went to the door, and knocked. Immediately, Colt started barking from inside. She remembered the last time she knocked on this door and heard the dog barking. It was the first night she arrived and was lost. Little did she know then how this wonderful bluegrass country would change her.

The door opened, and Jake stood there next to another man, who was putting his coat on.

"Mr. Duncan, you're making a mistake by not taking our offer," he said.

"I don't think I am," Jake replied. "If you don't mind, I have a guest."

The man stared at Karri and then walked past her. Colt ran out the door and stood at the edge of the porch barking as the man got into his car and left.

"Hi, come inside out of that cold," Jake said.

"It's pretty nippy tonight, especially for this California body." She entered the house with Colt following her.

Jake helped her off with her coat and hung it on a hook by the door. "Go warm yourself by the fireplace. I've got just the drink to warm you right up."

She walked over to the fire. The heat felt good on her face and hands. Colt stood next to her. "I bet this is your favorite spot on a cold night." She reached down and petted him.

"Actually, his favorite spot is right next to me in bed," Jake said., coming back into the room. He handed her a clear glass with a small amount of brown liquid in it. "Just sip this and you'll warm right up."

"Who was that man? He didn't seem very happy," she asked.

"It was nothing."

She took a sip of the drink and immediately started coughing. "What is this, moonshine?"

Jake laughed. "No, it's better. It's Kentucky bourbon, the best in the world."

Karri took a sniff of it and then another sip. "It's good. I hope you're not trying to get me drunk." More teasing, but after another drink she could feel her body start to warm, or was it because she was so close to Jake. "What smells so good?"

"Homemade pizza," he replied proudly.

"You mean frozen pizza made at home?"

"No, homemade pizza."

"Oh, made from one those of box mixes. Those are really good."

"No, I mean real homemade pizza. Come on, I'll show you." He took her hand and led her to the kitchen.

The touch of his hand convinced her even more that it was him and not the bourbon that warmed her body. The aroma of Italian cooking was even more intense once they entered the kitchen. He opened the oven door and took out the best-looking pizza she'd ever seen.

He closed the oven and set the pan on top of the stove. "I didn't know what kind of toppings you liked so I went with the basics, except I didn't have any sausage."

"A farmer without sausage? Isn't that unusual?"

He waved his finger at her. "You're stereotyping farmers. I'm a horse and cattle farmer, not a pig farmer."

"I hope that doesn't mean there's horse meat on that pizza."

They both laughed.

"No, no horse meat. It needs to cool a little before serving. Would you like to switch to some wine now?" he asked.

"That's probably a good idea. If I sip much more of this, I don't think I'd be able to drive home later." He took the bourbon from her and sat it on the counter.

"Oh? I'm going to have to remember that."

Damn, why did I say that, she thought?

Karri helped Jake set the table and he poured her wine. "Here, have a seat, and I'll get the pizza." He held the chair for her.

A few minutes later, he brought the pizza in and placed it on the table in front of her.

"This looks and smells so good," she said as he placed a slice on a plate and handed it to her.

He twisted the cap off of a bottle of beer. "I hope you don't mind, but I like beer with my pizza."

"Not at all. Next time, I'll take a beer too. Now, tell me what happened today when you and Tim went to that farm."

"They reimbursed us with no problem. They couldn't understand it though. I was the only farm they sold to that had complained."

"Maybe the other farms hadn't got to that hay yet."

"No, while we were there the guy called the other farms he's sold to. They'd all used the hay for their horses with no problems."

"That is strange."

"They're going to take some random samples to the lab to have it tested, just to be safe."

"That's a good idea." She took a bite of the pizza. "Oh wow, this is delicious. What did you do to make it so good?"

"It's the sauce. It's homemade."

"How did you make it?" she asked.

Jake dropped his head. "My late wife canned it herself last year before her accident."

"I'm so sorry." She placed her hand on top of his. "I didn't know."

He looked up and smiled. "No, it's okay. She would be happy that I'm serving it to you. I'm sure she's thinking it's time to move my life forward."

Karri withdrew her hand and took another bite. She felt a little guilty now having the thoughts she did about him. Maybe she had pushed him too soon without thinking about him still mourning her loss.

"You said on the phone today that you had an offer on Alma's farm. Are you accepting it?"

"I'm not sure yet. When I first got here, I couldn't wait to sell it and get back home. But, things have changed a little. I really like this part of the country."

"I'm glad to hear that, but you said something about being offered more than market value for it."

"Yes, Mr. Gilmore said someone wanted to buy it and was willing to pay more than the asking price. Is that common around here?"

"Yes, and no. Did he say who the buyer was?"

"He said he didn't know. The offer was made through a realty company in Louisville. Do you know something you're not telling me?"

Jake took a drink of his beer before answering. "There's a big company out of Louisville that's trying to buy up the smaller farms around here to make one big mega farm to raise cattle on. They are offering huge amounts of money. That's who that man was earlier. The money sounds good, but by the time the family buys a new home, there's only enough money left for them to live on for a couple years, unless they find a job."

"Is that a problem?" she asked.

"A few of the older farmers have accepted the offers and then retired to Florida. For the younger families, they sell their farms and then find there's no other work available. Oh, the big farm offers to hire them, but it's barely above minimum wage. Most of the farmers, including Tim and I have turned down their purchase offers."

"They want Tim's farm too?"

"They want all of our farms. After our parents passed away, Tim and I divided the farm in half for our own. This place has been in our family for generations. We're not about to give it up. We hope to pass it on to our children someday."

"My situation is a little different with me living in California. I can't live here full time with my bookstore out there. Besides, I know nothing about running a farm."

"A lot of the farmers that don't want to sell have formed an association to keep each other informed about offers from that company." Jake reached over and took Karri's hand into his. "It's important to us that we all stick together."

She felt guilty about wanting to sell now and lowered her defenses to let him comfort her. Then, a loud thumping startled her and she pulled her hand away.

They both looked for the source of the sound and saw Colt sitting by the front door, tail thumping the hardwood floor. They laughed.

"He needs to go out," Jake said.

"I should probably go home anyway," Karri said.

"So soon?"

She heard the disappointment in his voice. "I really should. I wouldn't want to be responsible for you to miss feeding your cattle first thing in the morning. I already did that once."

They walked to the door together, and Jake opened it to let Colt out and then closed it. He reached for her coat. "Let me help you with your coat."

"Dinner was wonderful, and the company was even better. Next time, my house and I promise not to sell until I talk to you more about it." She stretched up to kiss him, but he wrapped his arms around her to pull her in for a longer kiss.

"See you tomorrow," she said when they parted. It was pretty much the only thing she could manage to say.

Jake opened the door and Colt came running back in, nearly knocking them both down. "I guess he took care of his business," he said. Jake walked Karri to her car and she got in and left.

As soon as she walked into her aunt's house, she threw her coat on the chair and got out her cell phone to call Alex.

"Hello?"

"Hi, Alex. It's Karri."

"Hey girl. I was just thinking about you. When are you coming home?"

"I don't know. I'm not sure. Maybe soon. Maybe not. Oh, I don't know." Karri went into the kitchen and filled a cup with water.

"Are you okay?"

"I just got home from dinner at Jake's." She put a tea bag into the cup of water and sat it in the microwave and pushed the button to heat it. "I was telling him about the big offer I got on the farm and he proceeded to tell me about how terrible the company is that's making the offer and that all the other farmers will hate me, if I sell."

"He said they will hate you?"

"Well, not in so many words, but it was implied."

"I don't understand. Why would they hate you?"

"That company wants to buy all the farms here and make one big mega farm, but the farmers don't want to sell."

"And he was mad at you for considering the offer?"

"No, that's just it. He wasn't. He was comforting, very comforting, if you know what I mean." The microwave beeped, and Karri got her tea out, putting it on the counter while she got some honey for it.

"That sounds interesting. Do tell."

Karri took her tea and went to the couch in the living room and sat down. "It wasn't much. There was a really nice good-night kiss." She took a sip of her tea.

"Nothing more than kissing, right?"

"Right. Why? I thought you'd be thrilled to hear about that."

"Oh, I am, but Andy was telling me last night how much Brent is missing you and how he's changed."

"You're still seeing Andy? Alex, he's just as bad as Brent when it comes to women."

"You're wrong about that. Andy has been so sweet since we started dating."

"Believe me, you've not been treated like a lady until you've been around the men here in Kentucky."

"Karri, are you thinking about staying there?"

"Honestly, I wish I could. I really like it here, but I couldn't afford to be away from the bookstore."

"Does this mean you will be home soon?"

"I guess as soon as I figure out what to do with Aunt Alma's farm, I'll be headed home."

"I think you should sell the farm and come home now."

"Good-night, Alex." Karri hung up the phone. She feared that Alex had fallen under the Novak brothers' spell. She'd need to get back to California to talk some sense into her friend soon.

Karri thought back to that good-night kiss. Jake was a much better kisser than Brent and her thoughts wandered off to the bedroom. She wondered if Jake's skills in the bedroom were as good as his kisses. Her fantasy went a little too far and she snapped out of it when she spilled her tea on her lap. "What am I thinking?" She decided to call it a night and get some sleep.

Saturday morning, Karri walked through the farmhouse with the idea of maybe turning it into a bed and breakfast business. It would need some renovation, but she could visualize it. However, could she afford it and if so, would it earn enough money to stay afloat?

She used her cell phone to get on the Internet to research running a bed and breakfast. She also looked up the names and numbers of local contractors. It couldn't hurt to get an estimate for a renovation.

After about an hour on the phone with some of the contractors, she found out how much it would cost.

"You're the least expensive quote I've received today, but that's still a lot of money, Mr. Graham."

"That's my quote sight unseen. I'm going by my memory of Alma's home. If you're really serious about doing this, I'd have to come take a look at the house to give you a more accurate quote."

"I understand. It was just a thought I had. I'm afraid it's too big of a project for me to afford. Thank you for your time."

"You're welcome, Miss Taylor. Let me know if you change your mind."

"I will. Have a nice day." Karri ended the call and let out an exasperated breath. She would love to be able to keep the farm, but after her phone calls, it didn't seem feasible.

She had considered using her bookstore as collateral for a loan, but if the bed and breakfast didn't work out, not only would she lose the farm, but also her only source of income with the bookstore. Her only option seemed to be to sell the farm.

Karri needed to get back to sorting through Alma's things for donations, but decided she wanted to stroll out and take a look at the barn. Donning her coat, she walked outside.

She pulled open the door and stepped inside. The barn hadn't been used in years, nevertheless the smell of hay and horses still lingered. All at once, the first strong memory of being there as a child came to her. Karri and her dad were in the barn. Aunt Alma led a horse up to them, and her dad lifted her up and on the saddle. She smiled as she remembered how Alma led the horse around the barn while Karri held onto the saddle horn for dear life. Her dad walked on the other side of the horse with his hand on the back of the saddle to catch her, if she fell.

Karri looked up at the hayloft remembering the time she and her parents were leaving from a visit when little Karri ran from their car, into the barn, and up the ladder to hide in the loft to keep from going home. Her father had to climb up there to help her down because she found herself too afraid of falling to do it on her own.

"What are you smiling at?"

The voice startled her, and she turned to find Jake standing next to her looking up at the loft too.

"What?"

"What are you smiling at? Is something up there?" he asked.

"I was just remembering playing in here as a child and how it was both fun and a little scary."

"Yeah, that hay loft is pretty high for a city kid," he teased.

"What are you doing here? Is something wrong?"

"No, nothing's wrong. I tried calling, but you didn't answer. I was worried and came to check on you. I followed your tracks in the snow to the barn."

How sweet, she thought. "I must have left my phone in the house. What did you want?"

"Remember the association of the farm owners I told you about? I got a call that there's a meeting tonight and I thought you might want to go with me."

"I don't know. I'm afraid I'll get ambushed by them for wanting to sell the farm." She sat down on a bale of hay.

Jake sat down next to her. "That won't happen. They aren't like that. Besides, I won't let it happen." He reached over and placed his hand over hers.

The warmth of his hand conveyed his sincerity and the little squeeze he gave sent a spark directly to her heart.

She pulled her hand away and walked over to one of the empty stalls. "Sure, I'll go. I need to learn more about what's going on with this big company. What time?"

"I'll pick you up at six-thirty."

"I'll be ready."

§

THAT EVENING, Jake pulled up to the farmhouse and Karri stepped out and climbed into the truck. She looked beautiful, dressed in jeans with a brown turtleneck sweater peeking out from her coat. She wore her hair loose.

"Hi," she said after closing the truck door.

"Hi. You look great." The softest scent of vanilla reached him and he wished she were closer so he could take her all in.

"Thanks. I wasn't sure what to wear."

"You're perfect." He put the truck into gear and headed out.

"Where is this meeting?"

"It's at Bruce and Jean Parker's farm. A different family hosts each time. They'll probably have snacks and drinks, if you haven't eaten."

"Should I have brought something?" she asked.

"No, the host takes care of it. It's nothing fancy, just finger food. Everyone's anxious to meet you."

"They know I'm coming?"

"Well, yeah. I told them. Don't worry. They'll love you. Tim and Renae will be there too."

A few minutes later, Jake turned the truck onto a long gravel driveway lined on both sides with a brown wooden fence boarding some pastureland. They reached the house and got out of the truck.

"This farmhouse sure doesn't look like Aunt Alma's."

Jake let out a little laugh. "No, it doesn't. The Parker's tore down their old farmhouse several years ago and built this ranch-style house." Jake let Karri go up the walk first to the door, placing his hand gently on her back.

The door opened and a large older gentleman greeted them. "Welcome. We're glad you could make it."

"Bruce, this is Karri Taylor, Alma Carter's great-niece," Jake said.

"It is so good to meet you, young lady. Alma was a special person, and we sure do miss her."

"Bruce. Let them inside and close the door. You're letting the cold air in."

"Yes, dear."

Jake and Karri stepped in and found a petite woman standing behind Bruce.

"Hello, I'm Jean Parker, Bruce's wife. It's nice to meet you, and Bruce was right about Alma. We all loved her. Let me take your coats."

"Thank you. Aunt Alma sure seemed to have touched a lot of lives around here." She handed Jean her coat.

"How are you, Jake? I heard you had a scare with Chestnut," Jean asked, taking his coat and putting both of them on a bench by the door.

"I'm fine, ma'am, and Chestnut is doing really well now."

"Well, that's good. I think they're going to start the meeting soon. I've got drinks and snacks in the kitchen, if you want something."

"If you have some hot water and a tea bag, I'd love some hot tea," Karri asked.

"Bless your heart. I bet you're freezing with our Kentucky winter, aren't you? You come with me and I'll fix you right up. Jake?"

"I'm fine. Thanks. I see Tim and Renae, I'll be over there with them."

Karri went with Jean to the kitchen and Jake made his way through the people in the living room to stand with Tim.

"Hey, I wasn't sure you were going to make it," Tim said.

"I stopped to pick up Karri."

"Where is she?" Renae asked.

"Jean took her to the kitchen for some hot tea."

"If I can have everyone's attention, I think we should get started." Bruce stood at the front of the room. "It looks like a good turnout tonight, and I'm glad for that, but if you notice, we have two families missing. The Wagner's and the Reed's sold their farms and have moved away.

Jake felt someone at his side and saw Karri had joined him holding her cup of tea. Again, he put his hand on her lower back.

Bruce continued. "Has anyone else been contacted lately?"

"They were at my house Thursday night to make another offer," Randy Woodhouse said. "They upped their offer, and I told 'em I still wasn't selling and to leave."

"That's good, Randy. We all need to make sure we keep sending them on their way."

"They were at my house again last night, and I refused their offer again," Jake said.

"I have a question." Everyone looked over at Wade Haggerty, who sat on the couch next to his wife, who held their small baby. "Has anyone had any problems on their farms lately?"

"Like what?" a man in the back of the room asked.

"I've started noticing gas missing out of some of my machines on the farm. It started a couple weeks ago, and I thought I was imagining it, but then I started keeping track of when I filled them up. I checked them the next day, and a couple of the tanks would be empty and there were no leaks."

The people in the room began mumbling to each other.

"I had a batch of bad hay at my farm," Jake said. "I had it tested at the university's lab and it was full of milkweed. I nearly lost Chestnut to colic because of it. I checked with the place where I bought the hay, and none of their other customers had any problems. It just seems strange that my hay was the only one infected."

"I've got a few heads of cattle missing," someone else said.

"It looks like we all need to keep a better eye on our farms as well as each other's farms," Bruce said.

"What about the little lady there with Jake? What's she going to do with Alma's farm? It's smack dab in the middle of all of us," someone else asked.

All eyes went to Karri.

"Jake, maybe you should introduce her to everyone," Bruce suggested.

"Most of you probably already know who she is." Jake looked at

Karri, who blushed at the comment. "This is Karri Taylor; Alma Carter was her great aunt and she's here to get everything finished up on Alma's estate."

The room fell silent with everyone waiting to hear what Karri had to say.

"When I arrived here, my sole intent was to sell the farm as quickly as possible and get back to California. However, in the short time I've been here, I've come to love Kentucky. Honestly, at this point, I don't know what I'm going to do. There has been a very lucrative offer made, which I assume is from the same company that has approached all of you."

"What did you tell them?" someone asked.

"I told my attorney to tell them I'd think about it, but that was before I knew what was going on around here. I would hate to see Aunt Alma's farm in the hands of such a company."

"I think we are all going to have to work together to keep this company from taking over," Bruce said. "Everyone keep in contact with each other and we should start reporting these missing items to the sheriff. Take care, everyone and ya'll be careful driving home."

"There's still snacks and desserts in the kitchen," Jean called out. "Everyone take some home with you."

Jake and Karri waited next to Tim and Renae for the room to clear a little before leaving. Another couple came over to join them.

"Ma'am, I'm Wade Haggerty, and this is my wife, Liz and our baby daughter, Cindy."

"It's nice to meet you," Karri replied.

"We used to look in on Alma and just wanted to tell you how sorry we are about her passing," Wade said.

"Thank you."

"Are you coming to the school's chili supper tomorrow?" Liz asked.

"Chili supper?"

"I hadn't mentioned it to her yet," Jake jumped in.

"Of course, she's going to be there," Renae added. "We'll bring her, that is if Jake doesn't."

"Good. I guess we'll see you there then," Wade said before he and his family left.

Renae smacked Jake on the shoulder. "You didn't ask her yet?"

"I was planning on doing that tonight."

"That's not enough time. What if she wanted to make something for the dinner?"

Jake looked at Karri, who unsuccessfully tried to contain her laugh. "Let's go. I have something to ask you."

As they walked away, Jake could hear Tim and Renae laughing. Outside, he opened the door and helped Karri into his truck. He got in the driver's side and started the engine.

"It's going to take a minute or so for the heater to warm up. It might be warmer for you to slide over and sit next to me," he suggested.

She did and Jake put the truck into gear and drove off.

"So, there's this chili supper at the school tomorrow."

"Seems like I heard something about that," she said.

"Would you like to go with me?"

"I would love to go with you. What did Renae mean about bringing something?"

"Some of the ladies bring desserts to go with the chili."

"What time does it start?"

"I could pick you up around one-o'clock."

"That sounds perfect. I'll be ready."

Jake parked in front of Karri's house and got out to help her down from the truck. Snow flurries began drifting down around them as he walked her to the door. "Everyone loved you tonight."

"I just hope I can keep my word about not selling to that company."

"Things will work out."

They reached the door and he caught her by surprise when he took her face into his hands and kissed her, his tongue probing deep. She wrapped her arms around him and began kissing back. The longer they kissed, the more Jake felt himself becoming hard.

He lowered his arms around her and backed her up to the house. She had to be able to feel his arousal against her. He wanted to take her inside the house and make love to her right then, but as he was about to ask her to continue this inside, her cell phone rang.

"I'm sorry," Karri said.

Jake stepped back so she could get to her phone. He saw her glance at her phone and then rolled her eyes, but not answer the call.

"What's wrong?"

"It's Brent calling again."

"That your ex-boyfriend?"

"Yes."

"He's still calling?"

"I'm afraid so. He's a very determined man."

The thought of her ex-boyfriend still calling sort of spoiled the moment for Jake. "I better let you get inside."

"Oh, okay. Would you like to come in for a while?" she asked.

"I probably should get home. Colt will need to go out."

"I'll see you tomorrow then."

Jake waited until she got safely inside before he got in his truck and drove home.

CHAPTER SIX

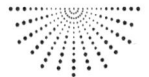

J ake knocked on Karri's door Sunday afternoon to take her to the chili supper. He got a little worried when she didn't answer right away and was just about to try the doorknob when she opened the door.

"Sorry I took so long. I was on the phone," she explained. "Come in. I'm almost ready."

He stepped inside and wondered if she had been talking to Brent.

"I need to go upstairs for my shoes and jewelry, and then I'll be ready to go."

She left and Jake sat on the couch to wait. He noticed her cell phone on the table and looked toward the direction of the staircase and then back toward the phone. If he could take a quick look at her call log he would know if she had been talking to her ex.

He started to pick up the phone, but stopped himself. What was he thinking? It was none of his business who she was talking to. Yet, it would only take mere seconds to look and he was only thinking of her well-being. She surely wouldn't consider going back with the jerk that she said Brent had been to her.

"I think I'm ready now," she said, popping around the corner.

Jake jumped off the couch. "Great."

She picked up her phone and put it in her purse and then got her coat from the closet.

"Let me help you with that." He held her coat while she put her arms through. "You smell like apples and cinnamon."

"That's not me and thanks for reminding me. I made an apple pie last night to donate today." She walked into the kitchen and came back out carrying the pie with a crumble topping.

"That looks so good. You made that last night after the meeting?"

"I did, and I might have made an extra one for somebody too," she teased.

"We're going to have to stop and get some ice cream on the way home later."

She covered the pie with foil and they walked out to the truck where Jake held the pie while she climbed in. "Why don't you slide over to the middle of the seat and I'll put the pie on the floor to keep it from tipping over," he suggested.

She did that, and after placing the pie on the floor and closing the door, he walked around the truck, proud of the way he got her to sit next to him.

He got in and they started out for the school. A few miles down the road, they came upon a church.

"What a beautiful country church," Karri commented.

"The cemetery behind it is where Alma and her husband are buried."

"It is? Can we stop? I'd like to visit her grave."

Jake turned the truck onto the narrow gravel road and parked between the church and the cemetery. He got out and she slid out behind him.

"It's back this way." He led her toward the rear of the cemetery passing several stones along the way and finally stopping near a simple headstone. Jake stayed behind her.

Karri stood there in silence for a few seconds before saying anything. "Hi, Aunt Alma. It's Karri, all grown up now. I'm sorry I didn't get here earlier, but I'm here now and I realize why you never wanted to leave Kentucky. I love it here. It's beautiful and so are the people." She looked at Jake and reached out for his hand, taking it into hers. "Jake Duncan is here with me. He's been showing me all around and taking good care of me while I've been here."

It was at that moment that the clouds moved east and a warm sun shined down upon them.

"I think she liked your comment about loving Kentucky," he said.

Winter had drained most of the colors from the artificial flowers on many of the graves, but Alma's grave, as were a few others, was bare of flowers.

"I want to get some flowers for her grave this week," Karri said.

"There's a flower shop in town. They should have something there for you. We probably should get going."

She looked back down at the grave. "We're on our way to the school's chili supper, but I'll be back later this week with some flowers."

Karri started to turn to go back to the truck, but a red female Cardinal landed on a newer stone a little farther back in the cemetery and started singing. Both Karri and Jake looked at it. Karri could see the engraved name.

"Is that your wife's grave?" she asked.

"Yes."

"Come introduce me."

Jake hesitated at first, but then walked back to Loren's grave. The bird flew to a nearby tree branch.

"Ahm, Loren, this is Karri Taylor. She's Alma Carter's great-niece and here to get Alma's estate settled."

"Hello, Loren. You sure have a great husband here, such a southern gentleman. Thank you for training him so well."

Jack laughed. "She always said I was impossible to train."

The bird in the tree started singing again.

"Come on, we're going to be late for the chili supper, and I'm starved," Jake said.

When Karri and Jake arrived at the school and walked in, they were immediately greeted by Renae, who was at the information table. "So, he did bring you," she said.

"He did and I made an apple pie to donate, if you need it."

"We can never have too many desserts. Come on, let's take it to the kitchen."

"You better make sure I get a piece of that pie," Jake called after them.

"Tim's over on that side of the cafeteria with Brian," Renae called back, pointing to the other side of the room.

As Karri walked with Renae to the kitchen, she looked around at the crowd sitting and enjoying their bowls of chili. A lot of kids were running around playing while trying to ignore their mothers' calls for them to behave.

"This is really a big crowd," Karri said.

"Yeah, we have a great turnout this year."

"This is a fundraiser for the art program, right?"

The ladies reached the kitchen and went inside to join the hustle of the women serving food.

"Jean, here's another pie," Renae called.

"What kind?"

"Apple."

"Oh good, we're almost out of apple pie. Bring it over."

Karri carried it over to Jean, who she had met the night before. "Here you go."

Jean turned around. "Karri, honey, you made this?"

"Yes, I did." Karri loved to hear Jean talk. She thought she sounded just like Paula Deen on television. She appreciated that last night Jean had spiked her hot tea with a shot of bourbon to help warm her up and not telling anyone.

"Well, bless your heart. Thank you so much."

"Jake made me promise to save him a piece of it," Karri said.

"It looks delicious, and we don't want to disappoint Jake. Why don't you take it over there to the counter and slice it for us? There's some plates to put the pieces on and keep one back for Jake."

Renae showed Karri where the plates were and grabbed a tray on the way. Karri sliced the pie and put a piece on each plate and then Renae placed them on the tray to carry over to the serving area.

"I didn't answer your question earlier," Renae said. "Yes, this is a fundraiser for the art department. With all of the budget cutbacks, my department always takes a big hit. But, the community is so supportive and helps all they can like coming here today, buying some of the art pieces from the students, or donating some money."

"This community sounds more like a family."

"It does feel like family a lot," Renae said. "I see Jake and Tim in line, we better get these desserts over there."

Karri looked over and saw Jake take a bowl of chili from the server and moved down the row to where she was standing behind the shelves of desserts.

"I believe you wanted a piece of apple pie." She handed him a slice.

"I did. Thank you."

"I'll get my food and come out to join you."

Both Karri and Renae got their bowls of chili and joined the men at the table. While sitting there, Wade and Liz Haggerty, the couple Karri met at the meeting, stopped by their table to say hello.

Renae finally caught her son, Brian who had been playing with his friends. "Did you eat some chili?" she asked him.

"Yes, ma'am."

"All of it?"

"Most of it." He tried to squirm out of her hold, but she had both arms around him in a hug.

Karri couldn't help, but notice that the mischief seemed to pour out of his eyes and face.

"Brian, would you like a piece of apple pie I made?"

His face lit up and a smile spread all the way across his face as he shook his head. "Yes, please."

Renae let go of him and he ran over and pushed his way between Karri and Jake. She slid her piece of pie she hadn't eaten yet over in front of Brian and he dug in.

"This is really good," Brian mumbled with a mouth full of pie and crumbs spilling out of his mouth and everyone at the table laughed at his forgotten manners.

A cell phone started ringing at the next table where Randy and

Missy Woodhouse sat talking with friends. Randy answered. "What? How bad? We're on our way." He hung up the phone and stood, looking at his wife. "We have to go. Our barn is on fire and it's spreading toward the house."

The Woodhouse's rushed out leaving everyone stunned, but it only took a few seconds for much of the crowd to jump up and follow them.

"We've got to go help too," Jake said to Tim. Both men rose from their seats.

"You're going to go fight a fire?" Karri asked.

"No, but they'll need help with their animals and getting things out of their house. Renae, can you take Karri with you?"

"Sure." Renae stood and gave Tim a kiss. "Be careful."

Karri also stood, but Jake was already heading toward the door with Tim rushing to catch up.

Most of the people who had been at the chili dinner had gone to the fire also. The tables were left with bowls, cups, and empty plates of desserts.

"Don't worry about Jake," Renae said. "He's the type of person who drops everything to help a neighbor. It drove Loren crazy."

The ladies sat back down at the table. "We stopped by her grave today," Karri said.

"Loren's grave?"

"Yes, on the way here today."

"That's kind of surprising."

"When we were driving by the church, he told me that Aunt Alma was buried there and I asked him to stop. While there, I saw Loren's grave, and we walked over."

"Wow, I figured he had developed feelings for you, but I had no idea how much."

"What do you mean?"

"Brian, go to the restroom and wash your face and hands and come right back here," Renae said.

"Yes, momma." He jumped up and took off running.

"No running, young man." She turned back to Karri. "Jake was devastated after her death. He closed every single person out of his life. It was only a short time before you arrived that he started coming out of it. You've been good for him."

"But, how good will it be for him when I go back to California?"

"I think he's hoping you won't leave."

"I wish I could stay, but my business is back there."

"We should get these tables cleaned off. If you want to help, I'll get you an apron?"

"I'd be happy to help."

"All clean, mommy," Brian said, running up to Renae.

"Yes, you are." Renae gave her son a hug.

Renae got two aprons from the kitchen, and with Brian rolling the trash can for them, they had the tables cleared and washed in no time. They took the trash to the janitor's room and left everything else for the kitchen staff.

"Thanks so much for helping," Renae said.

"It was my pleasure. I hope you made lots of money for the art department."

"We've actually had bigger crowds, but with the art sale and donation jar, we'll do okay. Are you ready to go?"

"Yes."

"Brian, get your coat. We're going home. Brian!"

Karri looked around and didn't see Brian anywhere. She and Renae started looking for him.

"Brian Duncan, you better show yourself right now," Renae demanded.

"I'll check the restrooms," Karri said.

"I'll look back in the classrooms," Renae said as she took off down a hallway.

A few minutes later, she showed back up pulling Brian behind her and mumbling something about him being the death of her. "He was in my classroom."

While Renae helped Brian with his coat, Karri fished a twenty-dollar bill out of her wallet and on the way out of the building she dropped it into the donation jar.

"You didn't have to do that," Renae said.

"Sure I did. Jake paid for the tickets for the chili, and I'm part of the community, at least for now, and I want to support the school programs.

"Thank you. It's much appreciated."

Renae buckled Brian into his seat and the ladies got into Tim's truck and headed onto the highway.

"The Woodhouse's farm is on the way home. We could stop by, if you don't mind. I'd like to see how bad it is," Renae said.

"That's fine with me. I'm concerned too."

Several miles down the road, they turned onto the driveway to the Woodhouse's farm. As they approached, they could see the fire was out, but smoke still rose from the rubble. Firefighters still poured water onto it.

"The barn's gone, but their house is okay. Thank goodness," Renae said.

Cars and trucks lined the long driveway. Renae parked behind a truck and they walked the rest of the way. The stench of smoke held in the air.

"Daddy!" Brian called, taking off toward Tim.

"Brian!" Renae called after him.

He ran full on grabbing and hugging his dad around his thigh. "Hey, buddy. I'm kind of dirty for you to be hanging onto me," Tim said.

Karri saw Jake standing with Tim and some other people. She and Renae joined them.

"Do they know what happened yet?" Renae asked.

"It was a field fire that headed straight to the barn," Tim said.

"A field fire? In February?"

"Yeah, it's suspicious, all right," Tim answered.

"Ada Mae, from the kitchen staff at school said she was going to bring some leftover chili for Randy and Missy. They certainly won't feel like cooking tonight."

"That's good. They'll appreciate that."

"I think we're probably done here. You ready to go?" Jake asked Karri.

"Yes."

"I've got cows and horses to feed," he added.

Jake and Karri headed toward the house where his truck was parked. Tim and his family walked back to theirs.

"I feel terrible that they lost their barn, but relieved they still have their house. Was anyone hurt?" Karri asked as they climbed into the cab.

"No one was hurt, and the neighbor that saw the fire got the horses out of the barn."

"That's good."

"They suspect the fire was started by that company that's wanting to buy us out."

"Can they prove it?"

"No. Unfortunately, it's only an assumption. There will be an investigation though." He looked over at Karri, who was sitting on the far side of the seat. "Don't you want to sit over here next to me anymore?"

"Not while you smell like smoke and horse manure." She pushed the button to lower the window a little to let in some fresh air, even if it was cold air. "You said you were going to feed your animals, would you mind if I came with you?"

"I don't mind at all, but I have to go home and shower first. I can't be around the horses smelling like smoke. It would really spook them."

"I need to change clothes too. Why don't you drop me off at my house to change and then I'll drive up to your house as soon as I'm ready."

Jake agreed and dropped Karri off at her house a few minutes later. "I'll be up as soon as I change."

"I'll leave the door unlocked. Just walk on in."

She closed the door and went inside to change clothes. She quickly dressed in jeans and a long-sleeved shirt and then remembered the apple pie she made for Jake and went to the kitchen to get it. After that, she went out to her car and drove to Jake's house. When she walked onto the porch, she found Colt standing there waiting to go back in.

"Did Jake forget he let you back inside?" She petted the dog and he responded to her with a bark. Karri opened the front door and the dog bolted inside. "Jake? I'm here," she called. No answer, so she took the pie into the kitchen and set it on the counter. She noticed some dirty dishes in the sink and decided to wash them for him. After finishing, she put the pie into the refrigerator since they would be heading out into the pasture. She opened the refrigerator door and heard someone behind her walk into the kitchen. She turned to find Jake standing there in nothing but a towel, water from his shower dripping onto the floor. He looked shocked to see her with his mouth dropped open.

"I didn't know you were here."

"Obviously."

"I forgot my clean clothes were in the laundry room."

He sidestepped past her and she could smell the scent of his soap from the shower. He moved into the laundry room and quickly closed the door. Karri couldn't help but giggle.

"You told me to come in when I got here. I called for you, but I guess you didn't hear me." The thought of Jake being naked on the other side of that door was enough to make her tempted to rush in there.

"No, I didn't hear you," he called from the laundry room.

"I was putting your pie in the refrigerator. We forgot to stop to get ice cream on the way home."

The laundry room door opened and Jake stepped out, now dressed in jeans and flannel shirt. "I was really looking forward to some ice cream with that pie too."

"I'm going to town tomorrow to meet with my attorney, I'll pick some up for you on the way back."

"Thanks. Are you ready to go?"

"Yes."

"Come on, Colt." He opened the front door and the dog rushed out first. He then let Karri walk out and they both walked out to the barn side by side.

Once inside, Karri stood in front of a huge tractor. Jake jumped up on it and opened the door. He held out his hand to helped her climb up and into the cab.

"I didn't know they made tractors like this," she said. The inside of the tractor cab was as fancy as the inside of her rental car. The seat was upholstered cloth and there was a radio with a CD player, but what amazed her the most was the heater and air conditioner. "This is amazing."

"Farmers like to be comfortable. You'll need to stand behind the seat. Sorry, it's only a one-seater. Hold onto the seat so you won't fall."

Karri moved behind the seat and Jake got in and sat down. He started the tractor and drove out of the barn to a wagon with three large round bales of hay already loaded on it. He backed the tractor up to the wagon and got out to hitch it up.

She watched as he skillfully went about his work, checking everything carefully before getting back inside.

"I think we're ready. Hold on."

He started the tractor again and with a bit of a jerk, they pulled away from the barn and headed toward the gate to the pasture. Colt followed at a slow trot. Jake stopped when he reached it. "I need to open the gate."

"Oh, let me." She climbed from behind him and he opened the door for her. Karri unlatched the gate and swung it open so Jake could drive the tractor into the field. Once he was all the way through she closed the gate and locked it. She climbed back into the tractor and took her place behind him again.

"You did that pretty well. I think you might turn into a farm girl yet."

"I'd love to go horseback riding sometime before I go back to California. Do you think we could do that?" she asked.

"I think we could, depending on when you plan on going back."

"I'll probably be here a couple more weeks." She hated to give him a timeline, but needed to get back to her bookstore and to her life in

California. Deciding to go back home wasn't an easy decision for her to make. She loved Kentucky, the people, and had developed quite a fondness for Jake, maybe even more than fondness.

"We'll have to watch the weather and the next decent day we have, we'll take the horses out for a ride."

"That sounds good."

Jake stopped the tractor and got out. He held Karri's hand as she climbed down. He handed her a pitchfork. "I'm going to need some help getting the bales off the wagon."

She hadn't noticed until now, but the cattle had surrounded them and a few were pretty close to her. "Jake." She had backed herself again the wagon and one particular cow was being rather inquisitive right in front of her.

Jake walked over to her. "They won't hurt you unless you scare them. They're hungry and when they see the tractor coming out, they know they're about to be fed." He reached over and petted the head of the cow. "Come on, give her a pet."

Karri slowly reached out and patted the cow's head and pulled her hand quickly back.

"See, they're gentle. But, don't come into the pasture unless I'm with you. You never know when a bull might not want you around. Come on, let's get the hay off the wagon."

Karri watched what Jake did with his pitchfork and together they pulled one of the large bales down onto the ground. They quickly moved out of the way so the cows could eat.

Back in the tractor, they stopped two more times to unload the rest of the hay.

"It's getting late, we need to get back to the barn and I still have to feed the horses in the stable," Jake said.

The sun was just setting over the horizon when they reached the barn. The farm looked beautiful with an orange sky.

Back inside Jake reached up and put his hands around her waist and lifted her down from the tractor. As their eyes met, he leaned down and kissed her. His lips were cool to the touch, but it warmed her from the inside out. Gentle at first, he deepened the kiss as his tongue slipped between her lips. Pulling her closer into his arms, he held her tight. Thank goodness for her heavy coat or he would surely feel her hardening breasts. Thoughts of them rolling in the hay flashed through her mind, but just as quickly as that thought came, a thumping sound interrupted them. They looked down to the ground and found Colt sitting by their feet again thumping his tail on a piece of plywood.

"Does he not like us together?" Karri jokingly asked. "He seems to always be interrupting us."

"I don't know. He's not really done anything like that before. Would you like to go out for dinner tomorrow night? It'll just be us, no family and no dogs." He looked at Colt, who laid down as if in shame.

"I would really like that." Karri remained calm, but inside she was doing somersaults

"Great. Oh, and dress up. I'm going to take you someplace real nice."

Thrilled that they were going to have a real date, she suddenly realized that she didn't have anything dressy to wear. She had nice clothes with her, but they were more business-type attire than hot date clothes.

"Karri, is something wrong?"

"What? No, why?"

"I've been talking, but you've not been paying any attention."

"I'm sorry, I just remembered something I need to do at home. I should go." She stepped out of his embrace and headed toward the barn door.

"Wait, at least let me walk you to your car." He caught up to her and opened the barn door letting her step out first. He took her hand into his as they walked to her car.

With the sun now below the horizon, the security lights around the farm were just starting to come on.

"It's really been a long day today and I enjoyed every minute of it," she said, opening her car door.

"It has and I still have to feed the horses."

"You work harder than anyone I know. I'm sorry I can't help anymore tonight."

"All the farmers around here work hard. We have to."

After last night and today, she realized how much these farms meant to the families. It made her decision about what to do with Alma's farm even harder.

"I need to go." Karri started to get into her car, but Jake turned her toward him. He cupped her face with his hands and gently kissed her lips and that warm feeling throughout her body was back again.

Jake dropped his hands and she got into the car and drove home. Once inside the house, she quickly located an old phone book and found the number she was looking for. She punched the number into her cell phone and waited as the ringing seemed to go on forever.

"Hello."

"Oh Renae, thank goodness you answered. It's Karri and I need your help."

"My goodness, what is it? Are you okay?"

"Jake asked me out for dinner tomorrow night and he told me to dress up." She paced back and forth as she talked.

"That's wonderful. What's the problem?"

"I don't have anything dressy to wear for a date. I only brought casual or business clothes with me. I never dreamed I'd be going on a date while I was here." Karri heard Renae chuckle over the phone.

"Don't you worry, honey. You've come to the right person. Tim and Brian are out feeding the animals. Let me gather a few outfits and things, and I'll be right down. See you in a bit."

Renae hung up and Karri sat on the couch. However, she couldn't sit still and got up to pace more.

"What am I doing? The main reason I came out here was to get away from a relationship," she said out loud. "And what do I do? I jump right back in. How stupid is that?"

Karri picked up her phone to call Renae and tell her she was going to cancel the date, but she stopped herself. She did like Jake and didn't want to hurt his feelings. "One date wouldn't hurt, could it?"

She heard a car door close outside and went to the window. Renae pulled several dresses out from the backseat of her car followed by a large quilted garment bag that Karri recognized as a designer bag. She opened the door to let Renae inside.

"Let me help you," Karri said.

"Thank you. I thought I was going to drop something."

"It looks like you brought a whole dress shop with you."

Renae placed the dresses over the back of the couch. "I haven't worn these in years, not since before Brian was born, but I think they should fit you. They're from the years that Tim and I went to the Kentucky Derby. You don't go there and not dress up."

"Let's go upstairs to the bedroom so I can try them on," Karri suggested.

Renae carried the garment bag while Karri picked up the dresses and they headed upstairs.

Karri had tried on her fourth dress when she stepped out of the bathroom for Renae to see. "What do you think?"

"I think that dark blue color looks the best on you of all the dresses."

"You don't think a shirt dress looks too casual?" She stood in front of the full-length mirror and turned to look at herself in the dress.

"I knew I forgot something when you tried that on." Renae unzipped the garment bag and pulled out a red belt. She walked over to Karri and put the belt around her, pulled up the dress at the waist to shorten the length, then adjusted the neckline to show a little more cleavage. "What about shoes? Do you have any heels?"

"Not that would go with this."

"That's okay. I came prepared." Renae looked at Karri's feet. "What are you, about a size six?"

"Yes, sometimes a six and a half, depending on the shoes."

Renae went to the garment bag again and retrieved a pair of shoes. She turned and held them out for Karri. "What about these?"

"Four-inch heels? Classy." Karri slipped them on. "They fit perfect. You don't think they're a little high?"

"You want to be taller so you don't have to stretch to kiss Jake.

Besides, look at your legs in them. Have they ever looked better? Jake may take you right there in the restaurant."

Both ladies laughed.

"Can you keep a secret?" Karri asked.

"Of course."

"The way Jake kissed me tonight, I don't think the dress and heels would make a difference."

"Karri, that's wonderful. He's been alone too long."

"That's just it." She came over and sat on the bed next to Renae. "I can't sleep with him. It wouldn't be fair for that to happen and then up and leave to go back to California."

"It wouldn't be fair to him or to you?"

It was a good question. "I'm not sure."

"I need to get home before Tim thinks I've left him. I think you need to wear this dress with the belt and heels and then make your decision at the end of the evening. See how it goes first."

"Oh, I know how it will go. That's the problem."

❧

THE NEXT MORNING, James Gilmore sat at his desk in his law office reading through a file when his secretary told him that Karri had arrived for her appointment.

"Thank you. I'll be right with her." Gilmore put the file in his desk drawer and went to the door. "Please come in, Miss Taylor."

Karri walked into the office and sat down in front of his desk.

"How are you this morning? Would you care for some coffee?"

"I'm fine and no thank you, I've had my coffee this morning."

"Very well. Have you made your decision to accept the offer on your aunt's farm?" he asked.

"Have you found out who is wanting to buy the farm?" she chirped back.

"Well, no ma'am. They're bound by a confidentially agreement."

"Mr. Gilmore, are you aware of the devastating things that have been happening at some of the farms around here?"

"I've read about a few things in the newspaper. Seems like that would be a good reason for you to sell and go back to California."

"The farmers' association believes that the corporation out of Louisville that wants their farms are responsible for the things that are happening."

"Now Miss Taylor, that's just a bunch of the good 'ol boys around here looking for an excuse not to sell. I bet they told you not to sell because your Aunt Alma's farm is smack dab in the middle of them."

"Yes, but--"

"And, if you sell, that corporation would put something on the property that would ruin the area. Am I right?"

"Something like that."

"I don't know if the company that wants your farm is the same one the farmers are talking about, or not. What I do know is that you're being offered far more than market value for the property and I think you should accept it and be on your way back to California far richer than when you came."

Karri sat silent for a short time and Gilmore hoped he'd made an impression on her about the farmers.

"No."

"Pardon me, Miss Taylor."

Karri stood. "I'll be going back to California in two weeks, Mr. Gilmore. I'll give you my decision about selling before I leave." She turned and walked out of the office.

Gilmore immediately picked up the phone and dialed a number. "Pete, it's Jim Gilmore. That Taylor woman just left and she still hasn't decided to sell. She said she's going back to California in two weeks and will have her decision by then." He turned his chair toward the window and watched Karri get into her car and drive away. "These farmers are putting ideas into her head. If you really want that property, you're going to have to get a little persuasive with her." He listened to the man's reply. "Right, I'll keep you updated."

***

Karri walked out of Gilmore's office more confused than ever about what to do. She sat in her car for a few minutes thinking back to the meeting a few nights ago at the Parker's farm. Everyone seemed so sincere. Were they really trying to put a guilt-trip on her? And, what about Jake and his brother and wife? Were they all just playing her so she wouldn't sell? She needed to figure out what was best for her, not necessarily for the community. She started the car and then it came to her. Shopping, I always feel better after some shopping, she thought. After putting the car in gear, she headed toward the highway and into Lexington.

With everything that had happened recently, she found it difficult to sleep and had done some Internet browsing for stores in Lexington. She pulled her car into a mall parking lot and parked her car in front of a lingerie store. She'd made up her mind sleeping with Jake would make saying goodbye when she left even harder, but that didn't mean she couldn't feel sexy all the way down to her undies. She got out of her car and walked inside.

It had been a long time since she had shopped for such intimate apparel for a special occasion. Not since she and Brent had gone away for their first weekend together.

A saleslady approached. "Is there something I can help you with?"

"I'm not sure. I'm needing some new undergarments for tonight."

"Something special to surprise the man in your life?"

"Not exactly. Just something to make me feel a little sexy while on our first date together." Karri could feel her face grow a little warm and she was sure she blushed.

The saleslady smiled. "I understand. Do you know what you'll be wearing?"

"Yes, a short navy blue dress with a subtle silver geometric print and red heels."

"If you'll follow me, I think I have the perfect coordinates."

Karri followed her to a table with a mannequin next to it wearing a red lacy bra and matching panties.

The sales lady held up the bra. "It has a plunging neckline for a no-show under your dress. The cup is lined with pockets for removable padding offering additional lift when inserted. As you can see, it has a lace overlay on the cups and a double row of hooks in the back." She placed the bra back on the table. "It also comes with a matching thong or brief panty covered with the same red lace."

Karri studied the ensemble on the mannequin.

"When he sees you in these with your red heels, he won't be able to resist you," the saleslady said.

"I don't plan on him seeing anything. This is more for how it will make me feel," she reminded her.

"Oh, of course."

Karri had a feeling the saleslady didn't believe her. Well, who was she kidding? She'd love for Jake to see her in these, and the saleslady was right, the heels would really set the mood. "I'll take the bra and the briefs." Karri selected her size and handed them to the saleslady.

"Wonderful. Is there anything else I can show you today?"

"No, this will be fine."

She followed her to the checkout counter. This cost so much more than she normally would spend, but it would be a nice souvenir to take home from Kentucky. She handed the clerk her credit card.

"He must be a pretty special guy for you to do this for your first date."

"We've spent a lot of time together, but this will be our first dinner date, and yes, he is kind of special."

Karri signed the credit card slip and put the credit card and receipt in her purse. The clerk handed her a small black shopping bag with the lingerie inside.

"Enjoy your date. He'll never know what he's missing."

"Thanks."

On the drive back to Willow Creek, she thought about what the sales clerk had said about what Jake would be missing. She had to admit to herself that she would love to feel the touch of his hands on her body, not to mention how his would feel. He surely had firm muscles and she would like nothing better than to rub her hands all them."

Suddenly, a blast of a truck horn revived her out of her daydream in time to bring her car back into her lane. "Okay Karri, no more daydreaming," she said to herself. Before returning to her house, she made one more stop to pick up the ice cream for Jake.

Once back at the farm, she fixed herself a little lunch and read her email. Alex had emailed again about Brent and how much he had changed and he missed her. She wondered how much of that was true and how much of it was Brent and Andy trying to convince Alex of it. She emailed back telling Alex that she had a date with Jake tonight and had just bought new lingerie for it. She knew Alex would tell Brent and Andy about the email. "Two can play this game."

Karri finished the dishes from breakfast and tidied up the living room before sitting down to read a magazine.

A few hours later, she took her bag of lingerie upstairs and laid her clothes for the evening out on the bed. In the bathroom, she ran water into the claw-foot bathtub for a bubble bath. The soak in the warm, bubbly water relaxed her so much, she nearly fell asleep.

As the water began to cool and the time for Jake to pick her up began to near, she stepped out of the tub and wrapped a huge towel around her. She walked into the bedroom and stared at the red panties and bra on the bed. "What was I thinking?"

She dried off. "Well, I spent a small fortune on these, I might as well wear them." She slipped on the panties and bra and turning side to side, looked at herself in the mirror. "Not bad."

She pulled the dress down over her head and smoothed it before placing the belt around her waist to shorten the length. "I'm going to freeze in this."

Checking the clock, she had just enough time to touch up her makeup and hair. She grabbed her heels and headed downstairs.

CHAPTER SEVEN

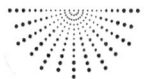

J ake opened the door to his house to leave and Colt dashed
inside. He reached down to pet the dog. "Be good tonight. I'll
be home late."

Outside, he got into his truck and drove to pick up Karri.
When he reached her house a few minutes later, before he had a
chance to get out of the truck, she came out of the house and
climbed in.

"Good evening," she said.

"Good evening. You must be hungry." He put the truck into gear
and drove up the driveway to the main road.

"Why do you say that?"

"You came out of the house so fast, you didn't even wait for me to
come to the door."

"Oh that. It's so cold out, I didn't want you to have to get out in it."

The smell of her vanilla shampoo drifted in the air. He loved her
scent and she looked great. At least what he could see of her did. Her
coat was buttoned closed and she wore a scarf around her neck. The
only part of her body not covered was her legs, her long sleek legs.
She hadn't lost her California tan yet and all Jake could think about

was starting at her toes and working his way up until he pleasured her like she'd never been pleasured before.

"Jake."

He shook his head to clear that thought. "What?"

"I asked where are we dining tonight?"

"There's a Latin American restaurant in Lexington called *Alejandro's*. The food is unbelievable. I haven't been there in a while, so I'm looking forward to taking you there."

"That sounds wonderful. I love Latin American food."

The drive to Lexington went by quickly. Jake parked the truck and rushed around to open the door and help Karri out. Once inside the restaurant, they were shown to their table. Latin American music filled the room as well as the sound of the other patrons talking.

Jake helped her off with her coat. As he did her dress slipped off of her shoulder, revealing a bright red lacy bra strap. His heart suddenly felt as though it was in his throat and he swallowed hard.

She instantly pulled the shoulder of her dress back up and turned to face him, smiling. Her eyes were like glistening stars and her skin so touchable, it seemed to invite him to see how soft it was, but he held back. He continued his gaze down the plunging neckline to her pert breasts and seductive curves. He looked back up. "Wow."

"You like?" She spun around.

He watched her twirl and felt himself becoming hard. "I do like."

He quickly needed to sit down, or the whole restaurant would know just how much he liked. Pulling her chair out, she took her seat. He placed her coat on the vacant chair and sat to her left.

The waiter had approached. "Would you care for a cocktail?"

Jake looked to Karri to let her order first.

"I'd like a margarita on the rocks with a salted rim, please."

"I'll take a Highball with an extra shot of bourbon."

"I'll bring them right over. Thank you." The waiter left.

The evening went perfectly. Over dinner, Karri told him about running a bookstore and living in California.

"I don't know, Karri. I don't think I'd like having to worry about earthquakes all the time if I lived there."

She laughed. "It's really no different than worrying about a tornado or a snow storm here." The waiter brought their after-dinner coffee and sat the cups down in front of them.

"But, with either of those, we have enough warning to prepare."

"I suppose you're right about that, but we're always prepared for an earthquake."

Jake took a drink of his coffee. "Have you made your decision about what to do with Alma's farm?"

"I just can't afford to keep it. I wish I could, but the maintenance alone would bankrupt me. On the other hand I don't want that big company taking it either. I talked to Mr. Gilmore about it today. He urged me to sell and sell now."

"You know, Jim Gilmore isn't the most reputable attorney around."

"I sort of got that impression, but he's the attorney that Aunt Alma chose to do her will and handle the legal affairs of the estate. I'm so stressed over all of this. I don't want to feel like I'm letting the neighbors down."

Jake reached over and took her hand. "You can't think that way. We'll all survive if you sell." He gave her hand a squeeze and Karri smiled.

"Are you ready to go home?" he asked.

"Yes, we should probably go. You have to get up early in the morning, right?"

"Yeah, those animals aren't going to feed themselves."

Jake paid their bill and helped Karri on with her coat. They stepped outside to find the weather had changed since they had arrived earlier.

"It's snowing. I love seeing it snow," Karri said. "Can we take a walk in it before we leave?"

She was like a schoolgirl. "Sure." Jake took her hand and they strolled down the sidewalk that ran along several storefronts next to the restaurant. Eventually, he put his arm around her and pulled her closer while they continued their walk.

"I'm going to miss Kentucky after I leave. It's so different here than

California. Don't get me wrong, people are nice there, but people here make you feel, well, like a part of their family."

"We are a friendly bunch."

They reached the end of the block and turned to walk back.

"I'll be leaving in two weeks. I have to get back to my store. I've been gone too long as it is already."

His heart ached at the thought of her leaving. He knew he didn't have the right to ask her to stay, but he hadn't felt this way about a woman since he first met his late wife.

He stopped walking and turned her to face him. "I'm going to miss you when you're gone." He held her face in his hands and leaned down to kiss her.

He gently touched her cold lips. Then deepened the kiss, dropping his arms he embraced her. She didn't back away. In fact, she reached up and put her arms around his neck and parted her lips allowing his tongue to slip in.

He pulled her against his body and against his hardening bulge. She must have felt it, just as he could feel her firm breasts against his chest, even though her coat.

Not wanting this to go any further on a public street, he broke the embrace, but grasped her hands. "The snow is starting to come down a little more. We should start back."

"You're probably right."

They walked hand-in-hand to his truck where he helped her inside. Once he got in, he started the engine and turned on the heater. "It will take a few minutes to warm up in here."

Karri held her hands in front of her mouth puffing hot air on them. "I can't believe how cold I suddenly am." She fumbled through her coat pockets and then in her purse. "I must have forgotten my gloves."

Jake drove the truck out on the slightly snow-covered road. "You can move over next to me and warm up. I can hold your hands in mine." He held up his right hand.

"I'll be fine. From the way the road is looking, you probably need to keep both hands on the wheel."

"Darlin', you're going to freeze if you don't at least cover those gorgeous legs." He reached in the backseat and pulled a blanket up for her. "It might have a few dog hairs on it, but it'll warm you right up."

"Thank you." She placed the blanket over her lap and legs. "I guess wearing a dress in this weather wasn't the best idea."

"Maybe not, but you had the attention of every man in that restaurant, including me, when I removed your coat."

She didn't say anything, but he could see from the dim dashboard lights that she was smiling.

The nearer they got to home, the worse the road conditions became. Once they exited the interstate highway, Jake had to shift the truck into four-wheel drive. He could see Karri had a tight grip on the door of the truck. He felt totally in control, but with her being from California, she wasn't used to traveling on slick roads.

The snow covered roads made driving to Willow Creek take almost twice as long as normal. By eleven o'clock, he parked the truck in front of her house. "We made it," he said.

"That was definitely a drive to tell my friends about back home." She removed the blanket and put it in the backseat. "I should get inside." She started to open the door.

"Wait. You can't walk to your door in those shoes. You'll fall in the snow for sure."

He jumped out of the truck and rushed around to her side of the truck. She opened the door and before she could set one heel down in the snow, Jake had lifted her into his arms and held her close.

"What are you doing? Put me down." She tried to hold in her laugh, but failed terribly.

"There's three inches of snow on the ground."

"Perhaps, you should take me to the porch then."

Jake carried her up the sidewalk and put her down on the porch.

The awkward moment commenced.

"The snow is really coming down," she said.

"Yep, the weather people sure missed this forecast."

"I really had a great time tonight. Dinner was wonderful."

"I had a great time too." He could see her shivering. She had to be cold with those bare legs, those beautiful bare legs. He couldn't wait any longer and took her into his arms for a kiss. She fit so perfectly against his body, as if she were meant to be there.

She wrapped her left arm around his neck and the fingers of her right hand intertwined in his thick hair. The kiss lasted until he felt her shiver again.

He broke off the kiss, their foreheads rested together. "Maybe we should take this inside," he suggested.

She dropped her arms and looked down for a few seconds before lifting her head up and looking into his eyes. "I don't think that would be such a good idea."

She might as well have stabbed him in the heart with a knife. He took a step back. "I guess I'm rustier at dating than I thought or maybe things are different in California because it sure seemed like you were wanting the same thing as me." He turned to leave.

"No, Jake. Wait." She reached out and touched his arm. He stopped and turned toward her. "You're not wrong."

"What then?"

Karri folder her arms in front of her and stood nervously in front of him. "It wouldn't be fair to either of us if we slept together."

"I don't understand."

"I'm going to be leaving here soon and probably never come back. It wouldn't be right to start something that's only going to last for a few weeks. It would make leaving even more difficult than it's already going to be."

Jake took a step toward her, gave her a kiss on the cheek, and left without saying a word.

Disappointment and frustration rained over him as he drove home through the snow. He knew she was being sensible, but why would she dress like she did if she hadn't intended on sleeping with him? Once at home, he parked his truck in the garage and when he got out, he remembered what was in his pocket. He pulled out a condom packet. "Guess I didn't need this after all." He put the packet in his pocket and went into his house for a cold shower.

KARRI WOKE up early the next morning and felt cold. She could hear the wind whipping around the outside of the house. Once out of bed and dressed in a sweater and sweatpants, she headed downstairs. At the bottom of the steps, she flipped the light switch. Nothing. She tried a few more times with the same results. "What the hell?"

She walked to the couch and picked up the remote control and tried the television. It didn't come on either. "No power. That's just great."

Karri went to the window to look outside. "Oh, my gosh." A blanket of white snow covered everything, and it was still coming down. She looked at the rental car. "There must be six inches of snow out there."

The house seemed to be getting colder by the minute, so she went to the fireplace and placed a few pieces of wood on the grate and after several tries, finally got a fire started. She knew it wouldn't heat the whole house, so she closed as many doors as she could to keep as much of the warmth in the living room as possible.

She also filled an old metal coffee pot with some water and sat next it to the fire in the fireplace to make coffee. She put on some socks and her boots and brought some blankets and a pillow down from the bedroom. Once the water was hot enough, she made herself a cup of instant coffee. A little worried about the weather, she sat on the couch wrapped in the blanket when her cell phone rang.

"Hello?"

"Karri, it's Jake. I wanted to check to make sure you're okay."

"The power's out. I started a fire in the fireplace and closed off the living room from the rest of the house to keep it as warm as possible, but there's not much wood here."

"You know there's a generator behind the house, don't you?"

"No, I didn't. But, I don't know how to use a generator."

"I'll come back there and start it and show you how to use it."

"How are you going to get back here? The snow is so deep, it's nearly up to the bumper on the car."

"I'll ride my horse. He can handle the snow. Just give me time to get to the barn and saddle him."

"Okay. Thanks, and be careful."

Jake ended the call without even saying goodbye. He was probably still mad about last night, she thought.

Karri added a couple more pieces of wood into the fireplace while waiting for Jake to get there. She checked herself in the mirror. She hadn't even taken the time to brush her hair this morning and it looked a mess. She got a comb from her purse and tried her best to look presentable when he got there, but failed miserably.

When she heard a knock at her door, she rushed to let him in. His oil-skin coat and cowboy hat were covered with snow and it fell to the floor when he stepped inside. She pushed the door closed, but not before seeing that he had tied his horse to the porch railing.

"Looks like I made a mess. Sorry," he said looking down at the floor.

"That's okay. Would you like some coffee to warm you up?"

"No, thanks. I don't want to keep the horse out in the weather too long." He looked around the room. "Looks like you're prepared to live in this room for a while."

"Only until the power comes back on."

"Well, that could take a while in this storm. They've upgraded us to a Blizzard Warning, so the power crews are not going to be able to get out for a while. Let's go check on that generator."

She grabbed her coat and gloves and followed him through the house and out to the backyard, which was a blanket of snow. The wind and snow nearly knocked her down when she stepped outside. Jake caught her arm to steady her.

"The generator is over there," he shouted to be heard over the wind. Jake held onto her as they trudged through the snow to a wooden box at the corner of the house. When he lifted the lid, they found it empty.

"Where's the generator?" she asked.

"I don't know. It's always been right here. You go back inside, and I'll check the barn to see if it's been put in there."

Karri held onto the side of the house as she made her way to the door and was sitting next to the fireplace when Jake came back in. He removed his gloves and held his hands in front of the fire to warm them.

"Did you find it?"

"No. I think someone stole it. The gas cans Alma used to keep the fuel in are gone too. This may be another one of those thefts that are happening around the area."

"You think that big corporation is responsible?"

"Could be."

"What am I gone to do?"

"Pack a small bag of clothes. You can stay with me until the power comes back on. I have a generator, a gas stove and gas water heater. The woodstove and fireplace will keep most of the cabin warm enough for us to be comfortable."

While it was probably a good idea to stay at Jake's for a while, she wasn't so sure she could trust herself to say no to him again if it came to sleeping with him. It had been all she could do to turn him away last night. If he had pressed the issue, she would have given in for sure.

"I'm sure I'll be fine staying here, but thanks for the offer," she said.

"Are you crazy? There's a blizzard out there. The temperature is going to drop into the single digits tonight, and that puny amount of wood is all you have left." He nodded toward the pieces of wood next to the fireplace. "So, unless you plan on burning furniture to stay warm, you best be packing a bag and come with me to my house."

She stood stunned for a second. No one had spoken to her like that since she was a child. She hated to admit it to herself, but she found his take-control attitude rather appealing.

"I suppose you're right. I'll go get some clothes together." She started for the stairs.

"While you're doing that, I'm going to shut the water off at the valve for the house and turn on the faucets to drain the water so the pipes won't burst. You need to do the same in the upstairs bathroom," he called after her.

A short time later, she came back down carrying a designer cloth gym bag. "Is this too big to carry on the horse? It's the smallest I have."

"It'll be fine. Do you have a hat to wear?"

"No, but I have a scarf I can wrap around my head.

"That will have to do. Get everything on. We need to get going."

She put her purse and cell phone into her gym bag and Jake helped her with her coat. Lastly, before going out the door, he grabbed a blanket. Once outside, he brushed the snow off of his horse and saddle and placed the folded blanket behind the saddle. Jake got on first and hooked the strap of her bag over the saddle horn. He held his hand down toward Karri to help her up onto the horse.

She looked up at him sitting on the tall animal. With his oilskin duster and cowboy hat, he reminded her of an old western movie she saw before leaving California; her hero that rescued her from the storm.

"Put your foot in the stirrup and I'll pull you up behind me. Once you're up here on the blanket, take your foot out so I can use the stirrup."

She did as he instructed and once she was settled onto the horse, he gave it a little kick and off they rode. The horse moved slowly through the deep snow, which Karri guessed to be about eight to ten inches in spots.

Karri had her arms around Jake's waist and held tight to keep from falling. She buried her face into his back to keep the wind from blowing the snow into her eyes.

The trip seemed to take forever to her because the horse had to step slowly in the deep snow, but finally Jake stopped the horse. "We're here." He helped her get down and handed her bag to her. "Go ahead into the house while I put my horse in the barn. Colt will probably run out when you open the door, and that's okay. I'll bring him back in when I'm finished in the barn."

Between the depth of the snow and the blowing wind, Karri's trek to the house seemed to be at a snail's pace. As soon as she reached the door and opened it, Colt dashed out, just as Jake had said. She stepped inside and closed the door behind her, glad to be out of that weather.

After removing her coat, gloves, and scarf, she went to the fireplace to warm herself. Jake's wood stove, attached to the other wall, was burning and it warmed the whole room. Karri's stomach growled. She'd only had coffee for breakfast and the hunger pangs were setting in. She wondered if Jake had any biscuits and sorghum like he had brought her on her first morning in Kentucky.

She went into the kitchen and felt like she had struck gold when she spotted a few biscuits left in a pan on the stove. She took two of them and a sheet of paper towel and sat at the table where she found honey, but no sorghum.

She heard a door open behind her and turned to find Jake coming into the house through the laundry room. Colt followed and walked into the kitchen, promptly shaking the snow from his fur onto the floor.

"Colt. No." Jake called.

The dog slumbered into the living room.

"I'll clean it up." Karri grabbed more paper towels and began wiping the droplets of water from the kitchen floor.

"You don't have to do that," Jake said. He took off his hat and coat and hung both up on the wall of the laundry room before coming into the kitchen.

"Yes, I do. You've rescued me from the storm and I owe you."

He reached down and took her hand pulling her up to stand in front of him. His eyes fixed on hers. "You don't owe me anything. That's what neighbors do for each other."

His touch to her hand sparked more feelings inside of her. She licked her lips, but this wasn't the time to start anything. "I hope you don't mind, but I helped myself to some biscuits and honey. I haven't had anything to eat this morning." She sat back down at the table.

"Let me fix you some eggs and ham to go with that. You must be starved." He got some eggs out of the refrigerator, and she noticed the light came on inside.

"Is the power back on? Your refrigerator light came on."

"No, I have a generator that the refrigerator, freezer, and living room ceiling fan are hooked up to. The stove and water heater are powered by propane, so we can cook and have hot water." He broke the eggs into the skillet.

"What room will I be sleeping in? I'd like to take my clothes out of my bag. The snow on the ride up got it wet and I don't want my clothes to get damp."

Jake put two big slices of ham into an iron skillet and it sizzled when the meat hit the hot iron. "I'm afraid we'll both be sleeping in the living room. Without electricity, the bedrooms don't have any heat. You can put your clothes in the bathroom and let your bag dry by the fireplace. Just make sure you leave the bathroom door open so some of the heat can get in there. It'll help keep the pipes from freezing."

While he continued cooking, Karri took her clothes to the bathroom. The temperatures did feel much cooler than the living room. She didn't want to leave her clothes out in the bathroom, so she neatly folded and placed them in the closet. She took her bag and put it next to the woodstove and walked back into the kitchen where Jake had just put the ham and eggs on the table.

"Brunch is ready," he announced.

"Brunch?" She sat at the table.

"Isn't that what you call a meal between breakfast and lunch?"

"Yes, but it sounds funny coming from you."

"Why, because I'm a farmer?" He brought the coffee pot from the stove and poured them each a cup.

"No. I think of snobby people when I think of brunch, and you're not that at all."

"Well, thank you." His wall phone rang and he put the coffee on the stove and then answered the phone. "Hello." He paused. "Everything's good here. I've got the fireplace and wood stove crankin' and the freezer and fridge are running on the generator." He mouthed the name Tim to her. "Karri? Yeah, I checked on her. Someone stole the generator at Alma's. Likely, it's the same bunch that's be causing trouble at all the other farms." The long phone cord allowed Jake to walk over and get his coffee. "No, I didn't leave her back there in that cold house. I brought her up here to stay with me." He listened to what Tim replied and then turned away from Karri and mumbled something into the phone that she couldn't hear and then he hung up the receiver.

"What did he say?"

"He was just glad you were okay."

She knew it was more than that. Renae had probably told Tim about her needing a dress for the date.

"I need to go out for a while and check on the cattle and horses."

"You can't go out in that weather," she said.

"I'll be fine. I have to make sure the horses have enough feed and that the cattle are close to the barn so I can get the hay out to them. I'll be gone for a few hours."

"Can I help?"

Jake laughed. "No, you don't have the clothes for working in these temperatures."

"I guess you're right about that. Is there something I can do here at the cabin?"

"You might see if you can find something for supper tonight."

"I'd like that. Is there some way I can use the generator to charge my cell phone?"

"Sure, you can plug it into the socket by the refrigerator, but try not to leave it plugged in too long after it's charged."

"I won't. Thanks."

Finished with his breakfast, Jake took his plate to the sink, then went to the laundry room and put his coveralls on over his clothes, preparing to go outside.

"I'm going to bring some more wood inside for the stove and fire-place in case you need it while I'm out. There's also an FM radio on the shelf above the fireplace, if you want to listen to some music."

"Thanks."

Jake put on his hat and gloves and went out the front door to the wood stacked on the porch. He made several trips in and out bringing in several pieces of firewood each time while Karri opened and closed the door for him. Colt had gone outside on Jake's first trip, but by the last trip, the dog happily came back in.

"I'm going to head out to the barn and then to the pasture. I'll be gone for a while so don't get worried."

"Be careful."

"I will. I'm going to leave Colt here to keep you company. The snow is getting too deep for him to venture very far from the house anyway."

As he started to leave, Karri thought for a split-second that he was going to lean down to kiss her, but stopped himself. She closed the door behind him and watched out the window as he tromped through the deep snow to the barn.

Once he made it inside, she turned her attention to the wet mess on the floor that Jake made carrying in the wood. She looked at water and then at the dog standing next to the door. "Some of this is yours when you shook off the snow, you know."

The dog looked at the floor and then to Karri before walking over to his spot next to the fireplace.

"Typical male; let the woman clean up their mess."

Colt yawned and he put his head down to sleep.

Karri found a mop in the laundry room and cleaned up the floor. Since Jake wouldn't be back for a while, she took the opportunity to tour the house. Just down the hall past the bathroom were two doors. Each door opened into a small bedroom. Most likely for the children he and his late wife were planning for.

She opened the door across from the bathroom and looked inside to find Jake's bedroom. It was a man's bedroom for sure with the earth tones used in the color scheme. The room looked fairly tidy, except for the bed. Instead of being made, he had only pulled the covers up. She stepped further inside and laughed when she didn't find any dirty laundry on the floor, only a couple pairs of boots.

The closet door stood open, and she saw the suit hanging in there he wore on their date last night. She walked over to the closet and breathed in the scent of his cologne. Before she could let out her breath, she heard a moan behind coming from the bedroom door. She let out the breath.

Her heart skipped a beat knowing Jake had caught her snooping and even worse, sniffing his clothes. She turned, but instead of finding Jake, Colt sat at the door. His head twisted sideways looking at her as if puzzled by what she was doing.

"Oh Colt, you scared me half to death." Relieved, she walked over and petted the dog's head. "Now, don't you go and tattle on me. Come on, we need to see what we can find for tonight's supper."

The dog followed her back to the kitchen. After a quick search of the pantry, she found some spaghetti and a jar of sauce. "This will be perfect for dinner." She wished she could find some Italian bread to go with it. She looked in the freezer and found a package of hot dog buns. She'd have to improvise.

Too early to start dinner, she did at least get out the pots and pans she would need. Through the window, she could still hear the wind whipping around the house. The snow still came down heavy, although she thought maybe it had lessened a little since her ride to the cabin earlier. She didn't see any sign of Jake though.

Turning back into the kitchen, she washed the dishes from their brunch, dried them, and put them away. She unplugged her cell phone and walked into the living room, sitting on the couch. Colt still curled up in his spot by the fireplace, looked up at her. "Yes, I know it's cold in here. I forgot about the fire."

Karri got up and filled the wood stove and then put a couple pieces of wood in the fireplace. She sat back down on the couch and let out a big breath. "This country living is exhausting." She leaned her head back on the couch, closed her eyes, and promptly fell asleep.

She woke up startled by a wet tongue licking her face and found herself horizontal on the couch and Colt's tongue on her face. "Yuck." Quickly, she sat up wiping her face. She looked at her watch. "I've been asleep for three hours? Jake? Jake, are you back?"

Silence. He said he'd be gone for a few hours, but she was now getting a little worried and scrambled to the front window to look out. The snow had lightened to flurries, but the tracks he had made earlier on his way to the barn were completely gone. The thermometer on the porch showed ten degrees, which made her realize that the house had gotten cool again. Back to the stove and fireplace, where she loaded both with more wood.

Karri wasn't sure what to do about Jake. She had no idea how long it took to do whatever he was doing. Then, an idea came to her. She went back to the couch to get her cell phone and called him. From the corner of the living room, a phone started ringing. He had left his cell phone on his desk. She hung up the call.

"I guess I'll start dinner," she said to the dog. "If he's not back by the time it's done, I'll figure something out."

In the kitchen, she washed her hands and her face where the dog had licked her. She found an apron in the closet and put it on, then filled a pot with water for the spaghetti. In a smaller pot, she emptied the jar of sauce to start it to slowly warm.

Thirty minutes later, the spaghetti was done and the sauce hot. Jake had still not returned, and now she was worried. Colt had curled up on the floor next to the table. Even with his head down, his eyes were opened and watching her every move. "I could call Tim about Jake. What do you think, Colt?"

The dog jumped up and started barking. Startled, Karri jumped and then heard the outside door in the laundry room open, and a snow-covered Jake walked in, and Colt rushed out.

"Thank goodness, I was getting worried." She stood at the doorway but resisted the urge to throw her arms around him.

"I'm sorry. It took longer than I thought. I would have called, but I forgot my phone." He took his hat and gloves off and tossed them into the big sink in the laundry room.

"I know. I tried to call you and heard it ring on your desk."

Next, he peeled his coveralls down stepping out of them. He stretched them across the sink to dry. Colt scratched at the door and Jake let the dog back inside. "Something smells good." He stepped past her and into the kitchen.

His hair was damp from sweat and ruffled into a mess. She wasn't sure he could look any sexier. "I made spaghetti. I hope that's okay."

"It's perfect. I'm starved."

"I have one more thing to make, but it'll only take a few minutes."

"Great. Let me go wash up in the bathroom and I'll be right back."

He left the kitchen and she opened the bag of hot dog buns. It didn't take long before everything was ready. While searching the pantry earlier, she had found a tablecloth and some candlesticks. She set the table with them including water goblets and a bread basket. She lit the candles, which helped with lighting the room since the day was winding down.

Fifteen minutes later, she heard him come out of the bathroom and into the living room where he put wood in the stove and fireplace and then came back into the kitchen. "Wow, look at that."

"I hope you don't mind. I thought candlelight would be nice for dinner."

"It's very nice. Thank you."

"Sit down, and I'll get the spaghetti," she said.

Before he sat down, Jake put some dog food into Colt's bowl and then sat at the table.

"There's garlic bread in the basket," she said as she placed the platter of spaghetti on the table.

Jake pushed the towel aside to get some bread. "Well, look at that." He held up the bottom half of a hot dog bun that had been spread with garlic butter and then toasted in the oven. "It's like a little loaf of bread."

Karri laughed. "I like to call it the poor man's garlic bread. I fix it all the time at home when I make spaghetti for---." She abruptly stopped in mid-sentence, and Jake just stared at her.

"Make spaghetti for what?" he asked.

"Dinner. I use hot dog buns when I make spaghetti for dinner at home." She couldn't believe she almost said Brent's name and she was pretty sure Jake knew what she was going to say. He dug into his food without responding.

"What took so long outside today? You were gone for more than a few hours," she asked.

"I had to hand-carry square bales of hay to the pasture by the barn to feed the cows, but they didn't want to come in like they did with us the other day, so I had to ride my horse out to herd them closer to the barn. It took a while in the deep snow to get them up to the barn. Then I had to feed and water the horses in the stables. It took longer than I thought it would." He took a bit of his spaghetti.

The wind began to blow harder outside and it sounded like a few tree branches landed on the roof.

"The temperature's dropping. I had the radio on in the barn and the weather report said most of the snow has passed us, but the wind and dropping temperature will be the big problem now."

"How cold is it going to get?"

"With the wind chill, it will feel like it's around zero. I hope you brought something warm to sleep in."

"I hope so too." Luckily she had brought her sweatpants and sweatshirt to sleep in. "How about some dessert?"

"You made dessert?"

"No, but I saw you hadn't eaten the apple pie I made, but I left the ice cream at my house."

"I think I'll pass on dessert tonight. After dinner, I'll need to turn the generator off so get what you need from the refrigerator and then don't open it again until morning," Jake said. He got up and took his plate to the sink. "Dinner was great. Thanks for making it tonight."

"You're welcome. I was glad to do it to repay you for letting me stay here." Karri got up and started clearing the table. "Will the heat from the woodstove and fireplace be enough to keep the pipes from freezing in here and in the bathroom?"

"If we're lucky, they won't freeze. It wouldn't hurt to let them run just a little from the faucet tonight. We also need to keep the doors open to the bathroom and kitchen, as well as the cabinet doors under the sinks. That will let a little more heat around the pipes."

"I'll get the dishes done and put water in the coffee pot for in the morning, just in case they do freeze."

"While you do that, I'm going to bring in some extra firewood for tonight. Come on, Colt. You need to go outside while I do that."

With darkness now fallen, Karri moved the candles next to the sink so she could better see what she was doing. After putting the leftover spaghetti in the refrigerator, she finished the dishes and filled the coffee pot. Satisfied that everything was done, she walked into the living room.

Jake had finished bringing in the wood and he stood in front of the fireplace stoking the fire. He had turned on the battery-operated lantern on the table between the couch and the chair, which gave the room a cozy feeling. Karri sat on the couch and Colt came over to her. She petted the dog and wondered what the sleeping arrangement would be with only the one couch in the room.

Once finished with the fire, Jake leisurely walked around the room closing all the curtains. "This will help a little to keep the cold air out of the room." He did the same in the kitchen and then stepped outside to turn off the generator. When he came back in, he sat down in the chair in the living room.

"Here's a flashlight for you," he said, handing her a small one. "You'll need it if you get up to go to the bathroom tonight."

"Thanks. Will your cows and horses be okay out there tonight?"

"Yeah, they're pretty resilient. The cows are closer to the barn and that will help block the wind some and the horses should be okay inside the stable. I've lost animals to cold temps like this though. We just have to hope they'll make it through the night okay."

"I hope so too." An awkward silence filled the room with the only noise being the howling wind and crackling fire. "Jake, where will we sleep in here tonight?" There, she finally said it, although she didn't feel much relief afterward.

"The couch unfolds into a bed. You can sleep there, and I'll sleep on the floor."

Guilt hit her like a brick wall. "You can't sleep on the floor. It'll be too cold down there."

"Oh, so you want me to sleep in the bed with you?"

"Well, I, ahem." She was tongue-tied and didn't know what to say.

Jake laughed. "Don't worry. I have a pretty warm sleeping bag and a thick pad to put under it. I'll be fine. Besides, I wouldn't trust myself sleeping any closer to you."

Karri was glad the room was dark. She was sure her face was a bright red from embarrassment.

Colt, spread out in front of the fireplace, yawned and let out a big groan when he did.

"I'm sure Colt will keep you warm tonight," she said.

"I have a feeling he'll end up sleeping at your feet instead of next to me. He's taken a shine to you."

"When I go back home, I'll miss him as much as anyone else I've met here."

"I better get you a pillow and some blankets and my sleeping bag." Jake picked up his flashlight and went to a room at the rear of the house. Several minutes later, he reappeared loaded with pillows, blankets, a sleeping bag, and a thick pad of foam.

"Let me help you." Karri jumped up and took some of the blankets from him. "Wow, these blankets are really cold."

Jake dropped the rest of it on the floor. "This was all stored in a room that I have closed off. Lay them out close to the wood stove to warm up before putting them on the bed."

Karri unfolded two of the blankets and spread them out near the fireplace. Jake did the same with his sleeping bag.

"Do you think I'll be able to go back to the farmhouse tomorrow?" She sat back down on the couch.

Jake put a piece of wood in the fireplace and then sat down on the hearth and gave Colt a pat. "If the power comes back on, we might be able to get you back there. I imagine most of the area is without power, so it might take a few days."

"Oh."

"Surely, you aren't sick of me already."

"No, I didn't mean for it to sound that way. I'm grateful that you brought me here to stay warm, but I feel like I'm always imposing on you."

Jake stood and stepped over to the couch, sitting next to Karri. "Don't ever feel like that. You could never be an imposition."

The glow from the fireplace reflected off of his face. She saw his desire and she felt it too. If he'd kiss her at that moment, she knew she'd give in to him.

"Karri."

"Yes."

"I think we had better get some sleep. I have to get up early to tend to the animals."

She was glad the room was dimly lit so he couldn't see her embarrassment, and maybe little disappointment, on her face. "Of course, you must be exhausted from working out in that storm today."

She stood and got the blankets. Jake stood up and removed the cushions from the couch before unfolding the bed. Karri looked at the bed and then at Jake, who immediately turned his gaze away from her. She tossed the blankets and pillows on the bed.

"I guess I had better put some different clothes on to sleep in," she said.

"You take the bathroom first while I get the stove loaded with wood.

Karri went to the bathroom to change. He obviously took her rejection last night seriously, she thought. Could she have been wrong about her decision to not sleep with him? She definitely felt an attraction to him, but would it feel like a one-night stand if she slept with him and then left to go back to California? She had dated Brent for a couple months before sleeping with him and then chuckled at herself for thinking that. Look where she and Brent were now, no longer together.

She changed into the sweatpants and sweatshirt, washed her face, and brushed her teeth. After putting her clothes into the closet, she opened the door and walked back out to the living room. The room was dark now. With the lantern turned off, the only light came from the fireplace. Jake had spread the foam pad and sleeping bag away from the couch and wood stove. "Won't you get cold that far away from the heat?" she asked.

"I'm counting on it. When I get cold, I'll know I need to put wood on the fire. Are you sure two blankets will be enough to keep you warm?"

"I think so." She put the pillows at the head of the bed and spread out the blankets. She crawled under them and pulled the blankets up. She was cold, but wasn't about to tell him that. "Good night."

"If you get cold, make sure you wake me."

"I will."

"Good night, then."

She heard him getting into his sleeping bag and then the zipper being closed. Finally, Colt jumped up on the bed and curled up at her feet. She was thankful for him to be there keeping her feet warm.

CHAPTER EIGHT

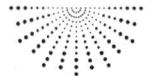

E ven with the curtains still closed, the sunlight lit up the room the next morning a little before eight o'clock. Karri heard a noise from the kitchen and sat up. Jake's sleeping bag laid open, empty. Then she smelled coffee, jumped out of bed, and raced to the kitchen in her bare feet.

Jake stood at the stove, fully dressed and flipping a pancake. He looked over at her. "You better put something on those feet or you'll get frostbite. The floor is freezing."

"Coffee first." She picked up a cup next to the stove and poured herself a cup.

"Cream or sugar?" he asked.

"A little sugar would be nice."

The sugar dish is on the table." He handed her a spoon.

She sat at the table and stirred the sugar into her coffee. "That smells really good." She took a sip and enjoyed the feeling of it going down.

"There's a few done already, if you want them."

"I do. I'm starved."

"Go put something on your feet first."

"Do you intend to hold those pancakes hostage until I put some socks on?"

Jake broke out into laughter. "I guess so."

Karri marched back to the living room and put on some socks and her robe. When she returned to the kitchen, Jake had placed a plate of pancakes by her coffee. She sat down and he came over with his own stack and another plate with bacon on it.

"Have some bacon too."

"Thanks. I love bacon with my pancakes." She put a couple pieces on her plate and poured the syrup. Jake then did the same. "What do you have to do today?" she asked between bites.

Jake swallowed. "Mainly, just check on the animals. I put extra hay out yesterday, but I need to make sure that none of the cattle wandered off or got stuck in a snowdrift." He took a drink of his coffee. "Did you sleep warm last night?"

"I woke up once when you put some wood on the fire, but that was okay, and you were right about Colt. He slept at the end of the bed and kept my feet warm all night." She looked around the room. "Where is he?"

"He went out earlier." He took another big bite of his pancakes.

"Won't he freeze out there?"

"Nah, he'll make the rounds as best he can in the deep snow. When he wants back in he'll scratch at the door."

After Jake finished his breakfast, he put his plate in the sink. "I started the generator back up this morning, so it's okay to open the refrigerator."

Karri finished and put her plate in the sink also. "I'll do the dishes."

"You don't have to do that."

"Yes, I do. I have to earn my keep while I'm here, remember?"

Jake's wall phone started ringing and he walked over to answer. "Hello."

Karri watched as a worried look swept over his face.

"How long has he been gone?"

She could only hear Jake's side of the conversation, but it was obvious that something bad had happened.

"Try not to worry, I'll be right there." He hung up the phone and turned to Karri. "That was Renae. Brian's missing."

"Oh no! What happened?"

"Tim went out to check on his animals this morning, and you know how Brian just seems to disappear all the time. She said Tim had been gone for about twenty minutes and she thought Brian was playing in the living room. She stepped in there to check on him, and he was gone, and so were his coat and boots."

"He went after his dad," Karri said.

"Probably so." Jake hurried to the laundry room and started putting on his coveralls. "Renae called Tim on his cell phone and he's out looking for him on the east side of the farm. I'm going to go search on the south side."

"I want to help too." Karri started for the living room.

"You can't go."

She immediately stopped and turned toward Jake, who now sat in a chair putting his boots on.

"What do you mean I can't go?"

"You don't ride well enough to take a horse out in the snow."

He was right. "I can't just stay here and do nothing."

Jake stood. "Renae is at the house by herself. Go get dressed, and I'll take you up there to stay with her."

Karri sprinted from the kitchen to get her clothes and then to the bathroom to change. In no time, she came back into the kitchen, putting on her coat, scarf, and gloves. "Let's go."

After adding some wood to the fireplace and wood stove, they headed out to the barn where Jake saddled his horse. He also placed an extra blanket behind the saddle where Karri would sit like he did when he brought her to his house the day before. After making sure the saddle was tight, he got on the horse and then helped Karri up. They rode to the barn door that Jake pushed open and they were on their way with Colt following in the horse's footprints in the snow.

The horse walked at a steady pace and didn't seem to be having any trouble except when they would go through a deep snowdrift. Karri held onto Jake with her arms tight around his waist.

After about fifteen minutes, she could see a house ahead of them and figured it was Tim and Renae's. It was a traditional looking farmhouse and even had a hitching rail in front to tie a horse onto. Once they reached the house, Karri slipped off first, followed by Jake who wrapped the reins around the rail. They both approached the front door, which Renae opened for them.

"Please come in." She closed the door after them. "Thank you both for coming to help." She broke down in tears and Jake hugged her, letting her sob in his arms.

"We'll find him," Jake said.

Renae stepped back, wiping her eyes. "I know you will. I just pray he's okay."

"Have you eaten anything?" Karri asked.

"Not since I fixed breakfast for Tim around six-thirty."

Karri placed her hand on Renae's arm. "Let's let Jake go out to look for Brian, and we'll see about getting something for you to eat."

Before going with Karri, Renae looked up to Jake. "Find him, find him safe."

"Don't worry, Tim and I won't rest until we find him."

Renae nodded her head and went to the kitchen. Before Jake walked out the door, he gave a long gaze to Karri. She could see it in his eyes. He was worried.

Jake left, and Karri followed Renae to the kitchen. Renae sat at the table and Karri checked to see if there was any coffee left on the stove.

"Oh good, the coffee is still warm. Do you want some?" she asked Renae.

"What?"

"Coffee? Want some?" she asked again.

"Sure."

"Can I fix you something to eat? You must be starved."

"No, nothing. Thanks."

Karri poured them each a cup of coffee and brought them to the table and sat down with Renae. In the short time Brian had been missing, she could see the worrying was already taking a toll on his mother. She needed to get her mind on something else, and Karri knew that wouldn't be easy.

"You know, I learned so much about being self-sufficient since I've been in Kentucky."

"How's that?" Renae responded, staring at her coffee.

"It's been a real learning experience to see how you, Tim and Jake prepared for the power being off. With your gas stoves, fireplaces, and wood stoves, you can survive for a long time."

"I suppose so."

Karri took a sip of coffee. "I bet you have a pantry full of home-made canned food from your garden, don't you?"

"Yes." Renae sat with her elbows on the table, fingers intertwined in front of her chin, and staring down at the table.

"How about I bake some muffins? If there's one thing I can bake, it's muffins."

"You bake?"

That brought her out of her trance.

"I'm better with pies, but I love muffins, and I bet Brian would love some when he gets home. What's his favorite?"

"When I want to treat him, I make chocolate chip muffins. He loves those."

"Why don't you and I make some for his return?"

"He would love that." Renae perked up.

"Good."

The two ladies got up. Renae started getting the ingredients together while telling Karri where to find the muffin pan.

"We can't use the electric mixer because the generator is powering the refrigerator and freezer."

"That's the way Jake has his generator set up too. So, we use a spoon?"

"I have a hand-mixer that we can use."

Renae dumped all the ingredients in a bowl and started turning the handle of the mixer until all the dry ingredients were moistened. "Here, you try," Renae said.

Karri did her best to work the awkward contraption while Renae held the bowl in place. Karri was quickly losing the battle of mixing.

"I think that's good," Renae finally said.

Soon, the muffins were in the oven, and the ladies went into the living room where they could sit more comfortably, but instead of sitting, Renae went to the window and looked out.

"I'm sure they'll call soon," Karri said.

"I hope so." Renae walked over and sat down on the couch. "I haven't talked to you about your date with Jake. How did it go?"

"It was nice and the food was wonderful."

"That's not what I meant. Did the dress work its magic?"

"It did. He loved it, but I sent him home after the goodnight kiss."

"Why did you do that?"

"I just couldn't do that to him. It's going to be hard enough to say goodbye to him when I leave."

"He cares very deeply for you."

"No, he's just taking care of a lost soul who doesn't know her way around the woods."

"I think you care very deeply for him also."

Before Karri could respond, Renae's cell phone rang and she quickly answered.

"Jake, what's happened? Did you find Brian?"

Karri saw tears swell in Renae's eyes and prayed they were happy tears.

"I'll be ready." Renae hung up the phone and looked at Karri. "Tim found Brian," she said between sobs. "He was unconscious, but alive. With the roads covered with snow, they're sending a helicopter. Tim is taking Brian by horseback to the highway and Jake is coming to get me so I can go with them to the hospital." She finally broke down and cried uncontrollably.

Karri moved over and let Renae cry on her shoulder. The timer went off for the muffins. "You need to get ready to go with Jake. I'll take care of the muffins."

"You're right." Renae wiped her eyes with a tissue and then got up to leave the room. She stopped and turned back to Karri. "Maybe I should take his favorite stuffed animal. He'd probably like that, don't you think?"

"I think that a perfect idea."

Renae continued out of the room and Karri went to the kitchen to get the muffins out of the oven. They looked perfect as she sat them on top of the stove and turned off the oven. She only wished Brian could be there to enjoy them. She put a clean towel in a basket on the counter and then placed the muffins in the basket. As she put the last muffin in, she heard the front door open.

"Renae. Karri," Jake shouted.

"I'm in the kitchen," Karri called back.

Jake came in. His face was cherry red from the cold. He had removed his hat and his hair was going in all directions.

"You look frozen. Would you like something to warm you up?"

"There's no time. I need to get Renae up to meet the helicopter.

"I'm ready," Renae said from behind Jake. "How's Brian?"

"I don't really know anything more than I already told you on the phone. When Tim found him, he called the Sheriff's Department for help and then he called me to come get you. We really need to go, or we're not going to make it there in time."

"Of course. Let's go." She put on her gloves and hat and picked up a small backpack that Jake helped her put on her back. They headed to the door with Karri following.

Before Jake went outside, he turned back to Karri. "I'll be back as soon as the helicopter takes off."

"I'll be waiting." She wanted to kiss him and if he hadn't turned so quickly to leave, she probably would have. "Be careful." She watched as Jake got on the horse first and then Renae, just as she had done when they had ridden there that morning. Jake gave the horse a little kick and off they went as fast as they could in the deep snow. Colt followed in the horse's tracks.

Karri closed the door and walked into the living room to sit down. Alone with her thoughts, she said a silent prayer for Brian's recovery. Her thoughts then drifted to Jake and what Renae had said, he cares very deeply for you. She couldn't deny it to herself any longer, she cared deeply for Jake too, but at what cost? She couldn't stay in Kentucky. She had a bookstore at home to run.

She also kept thinking back to what her attorney had said to her about the neighbors. Was Jake's motive only to save his and the neighbors' farms and not really caring for her?

The sound of a helicopter flying over the house reminded her of how Jake felt about family and how he had acted at the cemetery where his wife was buried. She didn't see how he could be the terrible person the attorney led her to believe about the good 'ol boys.

Her cell phone rang and the caller ID showed it was Brent. "Not now." She rejected the call. She thought back to Alex telling her Brent had changed and she wondered how true that was. He and Jake were so completely different. Jake, the proper southern gentleman, always opening the door for her, helping her with her coat, and even holding the chair for her.

Brent never did any of those things. However, he did have a few good qualities of his own. Expense was never a problem with him. He always took her to the best restaurants, had the best wines, and lavished her with gifts. Regardless, she wasn't sure it was enough. He had cheated on her.

Her cell phone rang again. She reached to reject the call again but saw it was Jake calling. "Hello."

"It's Jake. I got Renae to the helicopter, and they just took off for the hospital. I'm heading back."

"How was Brian?"

"He didn't look good at all, but he was alive, and the paramedics seemed hopeful."

"I suppose that's good."

"I'll be there in a few minutes."

Karri hung up her phone. She wondered what needed to be done before she left Renae and Tim's home.

Jake arrived a few minutes later and walked right in. Karri joined him from the kitchen where she had been putting things away.

Jake took his hat and gloves off. "I need to warm up for a few minutes, then I need to put Tim's horse in the barn before we head home."

"I haven't emptied the coffee pot yet. I thought you might want some."

"That sounds really good." He followed her to the kitchen where he got a cup out of the cabinet and poured himself a cup.

"Renae and I made muffins if you want one," she offered.

His eyes lit up when she uncovered the basket. Karri handed it to him and he took it to the table and sat down. She picked up a few napkins and joined him.

"Oh, Renae said for us to take these muffins home with us because they'd be stale by the time they get back home."

"I actually thought I'd put them in the freezer for them to eat when they do get home," Karri said.

"That's a great idea. She also said to tell you thanks for suggesting to bake them. It took her mind off of worrying about Brian, and she knew that's why you suggested it." He took a gulp of coffee.

"She was so worried, I was afraid she was going to bolt out the door to look for him herself."

Jake swallowed the last bite of his second muffin. "I could see her doing that too. Sometimes, she's worse than a mama bear watching over her cubs."

"Is that a good thing?"

Jake couldn't help but laugh out loud. "Oh darlin', you never want to mess with a bear cub when her mama's around. She'll skin you alive."

Now it was Karri's turn to laugh. "I love your witticisms."

Jake smiled. "Are you ready to head back to my house?"

"Yes, but I want to wash the coffee pot and your cup first. I'd hate for them to come home to any dirty dishes."

He picked up his cup and took the last drink before handing it to her. "What about the muffins?"

She went to the sink and poured the rest of the coffee in the pot down the drain. "If you don't mind, I'll put them in a bag and then in the freezer. I'll leave a note, so they'll know they're in there. They can thaw them for a snack when they get home."

"You really are too good to be true," Jake said.

Karri turned back toward the sink to start the dishes, she knew she was blushing and didn't want Jake to see her face. Suddenly, she felt him standing behind her.

"Here's my cup." His arm came around her as he put his cup in the soapy water.

She felt his warm breath on her neck and shivered.

"Are you cold?"

She hoped he hadn't noticed. "No."

Without warning, he turned her around to face him and kissed her. She didn't resist and put her arms, dripping with soapy suds, around his neck.

He ended the kiss. "Karri," he whispered.

Before he could say more, she stopped him. "Jake, we can't do that here, not in your brother's home."

"As much as I love what you're thinking, that's not what I was going to say."

"Oh." She widened her eyes and knew her face had to be flushed with embarrassment.

"I was going to say that you're dripping water down the back of my neck from your hands."

"Oh, my gosh!" She immediately pulled her arms back and tried to step away from him, but he held onto her.

"But, we definitely need to discuss your idea later tonight though." He kissed her one more time and then let her go. He walked out of the kitchen, and she turned back to the sink to finish the dishes. How embarrassing and she felt like a fool.

After finishing the dishes, Karri found Jake in the living room. "Is there anything else we need to do here before leaving?"

"I want to shut off the generator and fill the outside stove with wood. I'll put Tim's horse away, and then I'll be back inside."

Karri waited in the living room while Jake took care of the chores. She looked out of the window while thinking back to their earlier conversation. He wanted to sleep with her tonight, and she wanted the same, but at what consequence?

Why do I do this to myself? She lowered her head and then went to sit on the couch.

"Are you okay?" Jake had walked into the room without her hearing him.

"I'm fine. Maybe I'm a little tired, I suppose."

"We should get back home."

She put her coat, gloves, and scarf on and stepped outside. Jake closed and locked the door behind him. He got on his horse and then helped her up. They headed back toward his farm with Colt following, as usual.

Karri looked around the countryside on the ride back. The snow covered everything and even knowing that the cold and snow had caused Brian harm, she thought it was beautiful. She had her arms around Jake's waist to keep from falling, and he had placed his left hand on top of hers while holding the reins in his right.

When they reached his farm, he guided the horse to the barn. Once inside, he helped Karri slide down and then he got off the horse too. She stepped away while he removed the saddle and blanket.

"Would you like to brush him down while I get her some hay?" Jake asked.

"I'd love to do that."

Jake handed her the brush. "Brush the coat in the direction his hair goes. Start at the neck and work your way back, but stay away from his face, spine, and legs." Jake wrapped the reins around a pole to secure the horse. "Watch that he doesn't kick you."

Karri took off her gloves and began brushing the horse while Jake went to get the hay.

By the time she was finished, Jake had put hay into all of the stalls. He took the brush from Karri and tossed it into a nearby box. "Thanks for brushing him. He worked hard today and deserved to be pampered."

He unwrapped the reins from the pole and led the horse into her stall. Once he removed the bridle, he came back out and latched the gate. "We better get to the house. I'm sure both fires will be out, and the temperature is already starting to drop." He held his hand out toward Karri. "Come on."

She took his hand and they left the barn. The walk to the house proved to be difficult for her through the deep snow. She was happy that Jake held onto her hand or she would have fallen for sure.

Finally reaching the steps to the porch, Colt jumped around them racing to the door where he sat waiting.

"It looks like someone wants inside pretty bad," Karri said.

"He's not the only one," Jake replied, opening the door.

Colt dashed in first and went directly to his bed by the fireplace.

Karri started to take her coat off, but stopped. "Whoa, it is cold in here."

Jake went straight to the wood stove and checked inside. "There's still some live embers. I think I can get the fire going in there pretty quick."

He filled the stove with kindling and wood, and in no time, Karri could hear the fire crackling.

"Tim and Renae have an outdoor stove. How does that heat the house, if it's outside?"

Jake stepped to the fireplace and worked on the fire there next. "It heats water that goes from the stove into the house. A heat exchanger takes the heat from the water and uses it to warm the air in the house."

"That's too technical for me." A heat exchanger, she shivered at the thought of exchanging heat with Jake tonight.

"They only have to put wood in the stove twice a day."

He struck a match on the hearth and lit the newspaper he had placed under the firewood. "This should be putting off heat soon, if you want to warm yourself. I'm going to go out and start the generator."

Karri stepped toward the fireplace at the same time Jake stood up to leave. They got into each other's way and seemed to be doing a dance to let the other pass. Finally, Jake moved to his right and Karri moved to the opposite way. They both laughed as they moved past each other.

Jake headed outside while Karri warmed herself by the fireplace as the fire grew. She knew how difficult it was going to be to leave here. She had met some wonderful people, but too soon it would be time to go back to California.

"The generator's running. How's the fire doing?" Jake asked, walking back into the living room.

"It needs a little more wood, I think." She stood and stepped away so he could get to the fireplace.

"What do you want for dinner?" she asked.

"I was thinking of opening a can of beef stew. That would sure hit the spot on a cold night. I could have it ready in just a bit." He threw a piece of wood on the fire and replaced the screen.

"That does sound good. I'm going to go wash up while you get it started."

Jake headed to the kitchen and Karri dug some clean clothes from her bag and walked down the hallway.

Thirty minutes later, she came back into the living room, which was now lit with what seemed like candles everywhere, on the fireplace mantle, the stone hearth, the table by the couch, the bookshelves, and even his desk.

Jake walked in from the kitchen carrying two bowls of steaming stew and quickly sat them on the table in front of the couch. "I thought it would be warmer eating in here."

"Where did you get all the candles?"

"I like to keep candles handy for, well, emergencies. Sit down, and I'll be back with some drinks."

Karri sat on the couch and Jake came right back in with two bottles of beer and a platter of hot biscuits.

"I hope beer is okay. I didn't have any wine."

"Beer is fine. Oh, biscuits. You brought me biscuits on the first morning after I arrived in Kentucky." She picked up her bowl of stew and a spoon and gave it a stir before taking a bite. "You were right, this is perfect for a cold night."

As Jake was about to take his first bite, his cell phone rang. He placed the bowl on the table and answered it. "Hello."

Karri buttered a biscuit and watched Jake as he listened.

"That's great news. Thanks for letting me know." He ended the call and picked his bowl of stew back up. "That was Tim. Brian is awake and going to be fine. Well, that is until he gets home and gets his britches whooped for leaving the house like he did."

Karri laughed. "That's wonderful news. Renae was so worried about him."

"Oh, I talked to some of the firemen when the helicopter picked Brian up and they said the power could be back on as early as tomorrow. The weather report is calling for warmer temperatures too. It shouldn't take long for the snow to melt."

"That good to hear too." She took a drink of her beer. If the power comes back on, she could move back to the farmhouse, that lonely farmhouse. She took a bite of stew and glanced at Jake, who was concentrating on his supper. Typical man, she thought. She stirred her stew. What would she have done without him this week? She hated to even think about it.

"You're awfully quiet," he said.

She looked up and found him staring at her. "I could say the same about you."

"True. It's been quite a week, hasn't it?"

"Yes." Was he reading her mind?

He finished his food and placed the bowl on the table. "I thought I'd go check on your house tomorrow, make sure the pipes didn't burst in the cold temperature. You don't want to go home to a flooded house."

"Thanks. That would be a mess to have to clean up."

Jake yawned.

"Let me clear the table and do the dishes," she offered.

"I can help, but the dishes can wait until tomorrow."

Without warning, Colt shot up from his spot and raced to the front door barking.

"What is it?" Karri's heart pounded inside her chest.

"Something that shouldn't be there." Jake pulled on a pair of boots he found by the couch and got up. He took down one of the shotguns hanging on the wall and checked to make sure it was loaded.

Karri scampered over to him. "What are you going to do?"

He walked to the door and put his coat on. "I'm going to go see what it is." He grabbed a flashlight and opened the door. "Lock it behind me and don't open it unless it's me on the other side."

She nodded her head and closed and locked the door after he and Colt had gone out. It occurred to her that the laundry room door to the outside might not be locked. "Why on earth don't people around here lock their doors?"

She picked up one of the candles and crept through the kitchen to the laundry room and checked the lock. Sure enough, she found it unlocked and turned the deadbolt to the locked position.

Maybe she was being paranoid, but the thought crossed her mind that maybe someone had already come into the house through that door. Slowly, she turned and looked toward the kitchen door and screamed, dropping the candle on the floor and then realized what she saw. To the right of the kitchen door, a mop hung on the wall that, in dim light, looked like a person standing there.

Once she caught her breath, she felt like a fool. Fortunately, the candle went out when it hit the floor, but the wax had landed all over the linoleum floor. "Jake is going to kill me."

"Karri, Karri!" She heard pounding at the front door and went back into the living room.

"Jake?"

"Yes, open the door."

She unlocked and opened the door. First in was Colt, racing to his bed by the fireplace. Next, Jake stepped inside.

"Where were you? I thought I heard a scream." He took off his coat and hung it on the hook by the door.

"I went in the laundry room to make sure that door was locked."

He walked over and put the flashlight on the desk and his gun back on the wall. "Was it locked?"

"No, but I locked it. Then, I sort of made a mess."

"What kind of mess?"

"Bring your flashlight, and I'll show you." Jake followed her through the kitchen to the doorway. "I was holding the candle and dropped it when I thought the mop was someone standing there."

"I guess that was the scream I heard."

"I'm sorry about the wax on the floor. I'll scrape it up tomorrow once it's daylight."

He shined the flashlight down and sort of chuckled. "It's okay. You wouldn't believe all the things that have ended up on this floor. Come on, let's go back in the living room." He took her hand, and they walked back to the couch and sat down, still holding hands.

"What was outside?" she asked.

"I didn't find anything. I'll look in the morning when I can see tracks in the snow.

Jake then leaned over and kissed her. "I hope you don't mind, I just felt like doing that."

"It was nice." She desperately wanted to push him down on the couch and make love, but that would complicate things. When she felt him start to move toward her again, she noticed their supper bowls. "I didn't take our dishes to the sink. Let me clear the table. You're probably wanting to get to sleep anyway." She pulled her hand from his and stood. She picked up the two bowls and biscuits, but couldn't carry the beer bottles.

"I'll get those." He picked up the bottles and napkins, and followed her to the kitchen.

She put the bowls in the sink and Jake threw the empty bottles in the trash.

"I'm pretty tired. I think I'll go change clothes so I can get to sleep," she said. She left the kitchen and grabbed her clothes to sleep in and went to the bathroom to change.

CHAPTER NINE

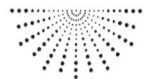

Sleep? Sleep was the last thing Jake had in mind for tonight. Was she teasing him with that kiss earlier today? "That woman runs hot and cold more often than the weather," he thought.

He went into the living room and built up both fires to warm the room better. "Let's see what she thinks about this." He moved the coffee table out of the way and unfolded the couch into her bed. He didn't want to seem too obvious, so he tossed his unrolled sleeping bag on the floor where he slept last night.

When she walked back out, she stopped and looked at the bed.

"I thought I'd save you some of the trouble," he said.

"Thanks."

"I suppose it's my turn in the bathroom."

"It's all yours."

First, he went to his bedroom to get some clean clothes and then into the bathroom for a quick shower. He placed his clothes next to the sink and then reached around the shower curtain to turn on the water. He retrieved a couple of towels from the closet and put them on top of his clothes. He started stripping off his clothes while the steam from the shower drifted around the room.

His thoughts were on Karri. She had pushed him away at least twice when he wanted to get close. Yet, he sensed that she was unsure each time she had. He didn't know exactly when it happened, but he had fallen in love with her. He adored her sweet face, her luscious lips, the way a sweater hugged her body accentuating every curve, and her jeans, oh how he loved the way her petite butt looked in her tight jeans. He ealized that he was becoming aroused and decided it was time to get into the shower.

He pushed the shower curtain aside to step in, and that's when he saw them, her red panties and bra. She must have washed them and put them on the handrail to dry. That was all it took, he was nearly at full erection.

Removing them from the shower and placing them on the towels in the closet, he then turned the hot water down and stepped in the shower letting the cooler water flow over his body hoping to tame his throbbing member. He soaped up his body and tried to not think about Karri. After rinsing off, he stepped out of the shower and quickly dried off. He was thankful that he chose baggy sweatpants to dress in since the cooler water had only partially helped. He finished dressing, ran a comb through his hair, and went back out to the living room. Karri sat on the edge of the bed petting Colt.

Jake walked over and sat next to her. "I'd like to talk before we go to sleep."

"All right." Colt moved to his bed by the fireplace, and they sat in silence for a few seconds. "What did you want to talk about?"

Jake took a deep breath and then let it out. "I think you know that I've developed feelings for you. Sometimes, I think you feel the same way, but when I try to get close, you shut me down, and I don't understand why."

She took a deep breath. "You're right. I am attracted to you, and I've not been fair by pushing you away, but I did it to keep from hurting you."

"I don't understand."

"Jake, I'm going to be leaving Kentucky soon and likely won't return. Would it be fair to sleep with you and then leave? It would be too difficult for both of us."

He reached over and took her hand. "It's too late. I think you hooked and reeled me in right after we met." He brought her hand to his lips for a kiss. "I was hoping you'd change your mind and stay in Kentucky, maybe turning Alma's house into a bed and breakfast like you talked about."

"I considered it, but it's too expensive, and then there's my bookstore back home. I can't afford two businesses. No, it's better if I leave Kentucky and go home."

She tried to pull her hand from Jake's hold, but he wouldn't let loose. Instead, he leaned over placing his other hand against her cheek and turning her head to face him. He brought his lips to hers. They were cool and that fueled his desire even more. This time, she didn't pull away. In fact, her lips parted allowing his tongue to slip inside.

Jake moved closer to her, moving his hand to her back. Her kisses were intoxicating, and he felt himself growing hard. Slowly, they both lowered themselves onto the bed, and his hand found its way under her shirt and cupped her breast. Her skin felt smoother than silk, and her breathing quickened as he circled her nipple with his thumb.

His kisses moved to nibbling her earlobe as his hand shared equal time with her other breast. At that moment, he felt her hands moving from his back to the bottom of his shirt and then underneath to caress his chest. Taking that cue, he began to explore her body with his free hand, slowing moving downward to her waist. His kisses moved back to her neck.

The farther down he moved his hand, the more rapid her breathing became. He felt her hand on his face as she moved his face so she could kiss his lips. Jake reached the waistband of her pajama pants and began sliding them down. A faint moan arose from deep in her throat.

Nibbling back on her ear, he whispered, "I want you, Karri."

"I want you too." She pushed his hand away and stood up next to the bed. She finished lowering her pajama bottoms and panties. Letting them drop to the floor, she kicked them away. Jake, reaching full arousal, licked his lips with his tongue in anticipation.

Slowly, she peeled her top off over her head and dropped it

to the floor. Mesmerized by her perfect body, he wanted to reach out and touch every inch of her. "My God you're beautiful." He stood and took her into his arms, capturing her lips again.

She broke the kiss first. "We need to do something about those clothes." She tugged at the neck of his shirt.

He didn't need to be asked twice, pulling his shirt off over his head. Her hands immediately went to his broad shoulders and moving down stopping on his rock-hard chest. The feeling of her hands caressing him nearly put him over the edge.

"I'll be right back." He raced out of the room, leaving her standing there with a confused look on her face.

Opening his bedroom door, he walked into the cold room. It felt like a freezer, but it did nothing to cool his excitement. He found the jacket he'd worn on their date and pulled the condom out from the pocket.

When he walked back into the living room, he found Karri on the bed waiting for him. She had only covered herself halfway with the blanket, leaving her exposed breasts glistening in the blaze of the fireplace.

He held up the little packet. "I had hoped to use this on our previous date. I'm glad I kept it." He started to remove his pants.

"Let me put it on you."

Her invitation nearly drove him over the edge, which became evident when his pants fell to the floor. He handed her the packet and crawled into bed taking her into his arms. "I'm not sure how long I can wait," he whispered.

"You won't have to wait long." She rolled over and straddled him.

Her hands cupped his unshaven face, and she leaned down to meet his lips. Her kisses moved to his neck, chest, and stomach. He'd never make it if she went any lower.

She stopped and sat up. She looked down at him with a penetrating gaze as she tore the condom packet open with her teeth. He swallowed hard knowing what was next. Her touch was gentle as she placed the tip of the condom on his aching shaft and began to slowly roll it down. Just before finishing, she leaned down and kissed the tip of his member.

That was all he could handle. She let out a little squeal when he quickly flipped her over and was on top of her.

She laughed. "That was fun."

"If you think that was fun, wait until you see what's next." He moved next to her, and with the tip of his index finger, he slowly traced a line from her chest down to her nest of downy curls. She shivered. Sliding his hand lower, she spread wider and drew in a quick breath when he found the dampness between her legs.

Jake couldn't wait any longer and climbed on top of her, entering her fully in one deep thrust. "Move with me."

Her hips rocked beneath him trying to match his rhythm. Closing his eyes, he let himself go. In the darkness, he could see fireworks and was seized by a rush of sensation so intense, he felt like he was on fire.

She raised her arms above her head, and Jake grasped her wrists and began suckling her breasts. Karri wrapped her legs around his hips and tried to keep up with him. His kisses move to her neck and ears. Finally releasing her hands, he rose up and slowed his momentum. Looking down, he saw a confused look on her face. "Don't worry, just a little treat for you." While still maintaining simultaneous motion, he stroked her with his finger.

She arched against him. "Oh, Jake."

He fell on top of her and ground his body into hers until he soared over the edge. Fireworks, there were those fireworks again, and then they were gone.

Collapsing on top of her, both gasped for breath. "Jake, I can't get my breath."

He rolled off of her and onto his back until their breathing slowed.

"Oh my God, I never expected a sensation like that," she uttered between short breaths.

Jake rolled over and cuddled her in his arms. "It was exactly as I hoped it would be."

"Really?"

"Yes." He gave her a squeeze. Content, that's how he felt. For the first time in years, he felt content and happy as he drifted off to sleep with Karri in his arms.

Jake woke up the next morning before dawn and carefully got out of bed. He put his sweatpants on and after relieving himself in the bathroom, he fed the fire as quietly as he could. He saw Karri's eyes blinking open and closed before she finally held them open looking at him. He crawled back into bed next to her.

"Sorry if I woke you."

She snuggled closer. "It's okay. Is it time to get up yet?"

"I'll need to get up soon to get to the barn. With the roads still being shut down, Marty can't get here to feed the animals, so I'll have to do it myself."

"I can help," she mumbled.

"No, you sleep in." He kissed her forehead.

"How did you sleep?"

"Much better in bed with you than on the floor in the sleeping bag."

"This complicates things, you know."

"I know, but we'll figure something out." At least he hoped they'd figure something out.

Colt suddenly jumped upon the bed and tried to lay between them.

Karri laughed as she moved to make room. "Think he's trying to tell us something?"

"I think he's trying to tell me he needs to go outside." Jake got out of bed and before going to the bedroom to change clothes, he went to the front door to let Colt out.

When Jake came back into the living room, Karri had folded the bed back into the couch and was sitting there waiting.

"I'm going to try and get the tractor out to plow a lane out to the road and also back to your house today. We're going to have to get out of here soon to get supplies."

"I thought you kept stocked up for emergencies."

"I do, and there's plenty of beef in the freezer, but we need eggs, milk, and bread."

"Of course. Are you sure I can't help with anything today?" she asked.

"You're always welcome to come down to the barn. The horses will need hay and water. You can help with that, if you really want."

"Sounds like fun."

Karri got up and went to the bathroom to get dressed. Jake was in the kitchen pouring coffee into a thermos when she walked in.

"Do you want me to fix some breakfast?" she asked.

"It's too early for that. Coffee is all I need right now." He looked out the kitchen window. "Wait until the sun comes up before you walk to the barn. I don't want you falling in the dark."

"I need to scrape up that wax mess I made last night first anyway."

He walked into the laundry room, stepping over the hardened wax on the floor, and put on his coat. "I'm going to go fuel the generator." He stepped out and breathed in the crisp early morning air. A sound coming from the front of the house caught his attention, footsteps coming toward him. Then, Colts rounded the corner of the house and sat at his feet. He petted his dog and let out a relieved breath before getting the can of gasoline from the nearby shed and filling the generator. After several tries, it finally started, and Jake saw a few lights come on through the window of the house.

After putting the gas can away, he went back inside with Colt at his feet. "Would you mind feeding Colt for me? I want to get down to the barn to check on things since we heard that noise last night?"

"I'd be glad to. Do you think someone was out there last night?" She got the dog food out of the closet and filled Colt's bowl.

"Nah, it was probably just a fox or coyote looking for food." He twisted the thermos lid closed. "I think I left plenty for you."

"Thanks. I'll come down as soon as the sun comes up."

"Great." Before heading to the barn, Jake took Karri in his arms and gave her a kiss. "It's been a long time since I've felt as alive as I did last night."

"It was nice waking up with you this morning."

Jake smiled. "See you in a bit." He left Karri in the kitchen and before leaving the house he stopped at his desk to get his handgun out of the drawer and checked to make sure it was loaded. Satisfied, he put it in his pocket. He didn't want to scare Karri, but he was worried that someone may have been outside the cabin last night.

Lastly, before going out the door, he picked up the flashlight. Locking the door behind him, he turned on the flashlight and looked around the snow. He could see where something had walked close to the house, but with Colt walking in the snow also, he couldn't tell exactly what.

He made his way to the barn and once inside went to the rear where a generator was located. He checked the fuel level and with one pull on the motor, it started, and the lights came on. The first thing Jake wanted to check was to see if anyone had been in the barn's office. He walked into the room and looked around. Everything seemed to be where he last left them. Still feeling a little paranoid, he went to the stalls to check on the horses.

Chestnut's stall was the first one. He was concerned about her since she'd had colic recently, but she seemed fine. After making sure the rest of the horses were okay, he took off his coat and pulled out the water hose to begin filling the water troughs.

About halfway through the watering, he heard the door open next to the office and looked around the corner to see Karri and Colt walk in. "How was your walk down?"

She joined him next to the stalls. "I tried to walk in your tracks in the snow, but you have a long stride."

He laughed. "Sorry about that."

"Can I help with something?"

Jake turned the water hose off and looked around. "You can use that pitch fork over there and move some straw from the wagon into that empty stall. I need to put one of the horses in there."

Before going back to watering the horses, he watched Karri get the pitchfork and use it to move the straw. She did her best to transfer the loose straw from the wagon to the stall, but failed miserable leaving a trail from beginning to end.

After finishing with the watering and putting the hose away, Jake came around the corner to find Karri proudly standing there holding the pitch fork in front of her. She looked like she was posing for the *American Gothic* painting, except she was smiling.

"Come see how I did."

Jake held back his chuckle at seeing her standing in what looked like a foot of straw outside of the stall. He walked over and looked inside. To his surprise, she had covered the floor with a couple feet of the bedding. "It looks great."

"Do you think it's enough for the horses to lay on?" she asked.

"Well, let's try it out." She squealed when he grabbed her, and they both landed softly in the straw. "Yep, it's enough." He leaned over and kissed her.

"You shouldn't start something you can't finish," she teased.

"Who says I can't finish?" He kissed her again. Her lips parted, allowing his tongue to sweep inside. He unbuttoned the flannel shirt she wore, and his hand quickly found her satin skin beneath her bra.

"I've never done it in a barn before," she whispered.

He smiled. "You're in for a new experience then."

Before he could do anything else, she stopped him and pushed him down on his back, straddled him, and unbuckled his belt.

Jake grabbed her hands and pulled her down on top of him and rolled over. He began kissing her while his right hand worked on her jeans button and then lowered her zipper when suddenly he heard the barn door open.

"Jake?" a voice called out.

"Damn it."

"Who is it?" Karri quietly asked.

Jake had already jumped up and was buckling his belt. "It's Tim."

Jake stepped out of the stall and around the corner before Tim found them together in the straw. "Hey brother, how did you get here?"

"One of the deputies brought me home in their military truck, and I drove the tractor with the snow blade down here. I'm surprised you didn't hear me drive up."

Jake heard a noise behind him and turned to see Karri walk out carrying the pitchfork. She had a few strands of hay stuck in her hair.

"I finished with the hay in the stall," she said. "Hi Tim, how's Brian?"

Jake could tell Tim was doing his best to hold back a grin.

"He's doing really well. If the roads are clear tomorrow, he can come home."

"That's fantastic news." She looked at Jake. "Since I'm finished here, I'm going back to the house to start breakfast."

"I'll be up in a little while."

"Tim, would like to join us for breakfast?" she asked.

"No, thanks," he said, smiling at Jake.

Karri left the barn and Jake looked at Tim. "Wipe that shit-eaten grin off your face."

"Little brother, I think it's great you two finally hooked up."

"What makes you think that happened?"

Tim burst out laughing. "The chemistry between you two became obvious long ago. Renae and I were even betting on when you two would get together. When you told me you'd brought Karri to your house after the power went out, we knew it would happen."

Jake nervously raked his fingers through his hair. "I'm really hoping she'll decide not to go back to California."

"I hope she stays too. She's been good for you and if she stays maybe she won't sell Alma's farm."

"Speaking of Alma's farm, someone stole the generator from the back of the house. When I went to check on Karri at the start of the storm, we went out behind the house to start it and found it gone."

Tim shook his head in disgust. "Any idea who took it?"

"I'd bet it's the same bunch that's been doing stuff to all of our farms to get us to get us to sell. As soon as the roads are passable, I'll take Karri to the Sheriff's Department to file a report."

"The roads should be back open tomorrow." Tim started putting his gloves back on. "I'll see if I can plow a path back to Alma's house so Karri can get home as soon as the power comes on. That is unless you don't want me to?"

"Get out of here," Jake joked.

Tim left, and Jake led Chestnut to the freshly made stall. After cleaning out her old stall, he walked back to the house.

Jake opened the door and stepped into the laundry room and the smell of bacon and eggs held in the air. He didn't realize how hungry he was until he smelled the food. Karri sat at the kitchen table reading a magazine.

She looked up. "All finished?"

"For now, yes. That food sure smells good." He stood in the laundry room and removed his coat and gloves, then washed his hands.

"I made a frittata. Oh, you're out of eggs now."

"Tim said he would clear the driveway with his tractor, so we can get out to get some groceries later today, and we should probably stop by the Sheriff's office to report your generator being stolen. You'll need a police report to file a claim with the insurance company." Jake came into the kitchen and opened the refrigerator door.

Karri walked to the oven and lifted an iron skillet holding the frittata out placing it on top of the stove.

"Where's the milk?" he asked.

"I'm sorry. I used the last of it in the frittata." She cut a serving from the skillet, placed it onto a plate, and handed it to Jake.

"We better make a list for the grocery store." He grabbed a fork and took his plate to the table. Karri dished the food onto her plate and joined him.

"I'll need to get some supplies too. I'm sure the food at Aunt Alma's has spoiled by now."

He got up to get some coffee. Disappointed that she mentioned getting supplies, he guessed she planned on moving back to her house. "Need a refill?"

"No, thanks."

He brought his coffee back to the table and sat down.

"Do you think Tim knew what we were doing in the horse stall earlier?" she asked.

Jake laughed. "I think he had a pretty good idea." He reached over and pulled a couple pieces of straw from her hair and showed them to her.

Her eyes widened. "I'm so embarrassed. How can I face him again?"

"Don't be. It's not like I've never caught him in the same situation before."

She jerked her head back up. "Really? Tim?"

"Yep, back in high school, and as I recall, he was pulling his pants and boots back on when I caught him and Renae in the hay loft."

"Oh, that's priceless."

After breakfast, Jake shoveled a path to his truck, and after getting cleaned up, they were able to drive to town.

"It looks like the highway has been cleared. I hope the trucks have been able to get to the grocery store to restock."

"I'm sure it has. The owners are pretty good about trying to make sure they have plenty of food after a big snow." He turned onto the street where the Sheriff's Department was located and parked near the building. He helped Karri out of the truck and over some ridges of snow along the sidewalk, and they went inside.

"Hello, Jake. I see you dug yourself out," the officer behind the counter said.

"I just did today."

"I heard Tim's boy is going to be okay. He's a lucky little fella."

"He is that."

"What brings you in today?" the officer asked.

"Joe, this is Karri Taylor. She's Alma Carter's great-niece. She inherited Alma's property after her death and is staying out there for a while. Karri, this is Deputy Joe Wright."

"How do you do, ma'am. I sure was sorry to hear of Miss Alma's death. She was a fine lady."

"Thank you," Karri replied. "It seems everyone had the same feeling about her."

"Joe, when the snow storm hit, I went down to check on Karri and start Alma's generator, but we discovered someone had stolen it."

"Come on back to my desk and we'll get a report filled out." The tall, lanky deputy walked to the end of the counter and opened the gate to let them through. He led them to his desk and they sat down.

140

"I'm thinking this is another attempt to drive the landowners to sell their farms," Jake suggested.

"Could be." The deputy opened a document on his computer and began typing. He asked Karri the usual name, address, phone number, and description of the generator. "When do you think it was taken?"

"I have no idea," she replied.

"No one has looked at it since before Alma passed away," Jake added.

"So, you really don't know if it's related to the recent thefts or not?"

"Not really, but Joe, you know that big company is doing all it can to drive all of us off our properties and sell to them. They burned the Woodhouse's barn down."

"There's been no proof that fire was arson," the deputy pointed out.

"Come on, Joe. You know it was arson."

"I said there was no *proof* it was arson." The printer behind the deputy came on and papers began coming out. He picked them off of the printer and placed them in front of Karri. "Look over the report and sign both copies on the bottom of the last page. One is for the department, and the other is for your insurance company."

She began looking over the document.

"What are most folks going to do about their farms out around you?" the deputy asked Jake.

"No one wants to sell, but when buildings start burning down, they may not have a choice."

"If we had more manpower, we could increase patrols, but it's just too much area for our small department to cover."

"I understand."

Karri signed both reports and pushed them toward the deputy. "Here you go."

Deputy Wright signed both copies as well. He folded one and put it in an envelope, handing it to Karri. "I doubt we'll recover it, but at least you can file a claim with the insurance company."

"Thank you," she replied.

She and Jake left the building and walked back to his truck. "The grocery store is next. Is there anywhere else you need to go while we're in town?" he asked.

"No, just the market."

The store was a mad house when they arrived. It took three trips through the small lot before a parking spot opened up. Inside was no better. They got the last shopping cart available.

"Is it always this bad after a snow storm?" Karri asked.

"Not usually, most folks keep a supply of food for emergencies, but this storm took everyone by surprise."

As they entered the produce department, an older woman who was restocking the tomatoes stopped them. "Hello, Jake. I see you finally made it back out into the world."

"Yes, ma'am." He took the woman in a hug and gave her a kiss on the cheek. "Helen, this is Karri Taylor. She's Alma Carter's great-niece. Karri, this is Helen Stanton." He paused. "My mother-in-law."

"I know all about Karri. She was the talk of the town before the storm hit. How do you do?"

"It's nice to meet you, Mrs. Stanton."

"Have you decided what you're going to do with Alma's farm yet?" Helen asked.

"I'm still considering all of my options."

"Well, I'm sure you'll do the right thing." She turned to Jake. "How is Brian? I heard he came home."

"Tim said he should be home today and he's doing fine."

"That's wonderful. Children are such a blessing." She looked at Karri. "It's so sad that Jake and Loren didn't have any children before her accident."

"Yes, as you said, children are a blessing," Karri replied.

Jake jumped in. "We probably should get our shopping done before the shelves empty again. It was nice running into to you, Helen." He grabbed the front of the shopping cart and started pulling it and Karri down the aisle.

"Once this snow melts, I expect you for dinner soon," Helen called after him.

Jake stopped at the big box of potatoes in the middle of the aisle and put a ten-pound bag into the cart. "Sorry about that."

"About what?" Karri asked.

"I forgot all about Helen working here."

"Are you sorry because I met her, or because she met me?"

"Neither. It felt a little weird talking to her with you by my side."

Karri put two sweet potatoes in a plastic bag and then into the cart. "She surely knows that you would eventually move on after her daughter's accident. Wait, she doesn't blame you for Loren's death, does she?" She pushed the cart into the dairy section.

"No, not at all, but you heard her. She regrets us not giving her a grandchild."

She picked up a gallon of milk and two cartons of eggs and put them into the cart. "What about Loren's siblings? Do they have any children?"

"Loren was an only child."

"Now, I understand."

They continued their shopping through the store, checked out, and loaded the truck for the drive home.

"What do you want for dinner tonight?" Karri asked as they pulled out onto the highway.

"I'd like to fix dinner tonight."

"Really? What did you have in mind?"

"I want to fry some chicken for you. I fry the best chicken in the whole county. Besides you can't come to Kentucky and not have fried chicken."

"Oh yeah? Do you use eleven herbs and spices too?" She teased.

"Better. I use twelve." He winked.

Karri laughed at his joke. "I can't wait to try it."

They drove back to his house and put the groceries away. Jake went to the barn to check on the animals again and then used the tractor to take hay to the cattle. Karri stayed at the house and tidied things up.

After dinner that night, they both finished the dishes together, and Jake went outside to fill the generator with fuel. Afterward in the living room, Jake started adding some wood to the fireplace and wood stove, and then he and Karri sat on the couch. She placed her glass of wine on the table next to her.

"I talked to Tim on the phone a while ago," he said. "He said he cleared the road back to your house today and we should be able to make it back there in my truck, but I'll have to dig your car out with a shovel. He said he did the best he could with the tractor."

"You've done so much for me, I don't know how I can ever repay you, but if you have two shovels, I can help too," she said.

"I'm sure I can use the help, but you don't have to repay me. That's just how folks help each other around here." He finished with the fire and came over to sit next to her.

"I heard on the radio that there should be a warm-up tomorrow that will start melting the snow," she said.

"Yeah, the power should be back on tomorrow too."

It was nervous talk with neither one not sure what to say to each other. Then, at the same time, they both started to speak.

"Oh, sorry, you go ahead," Karri said.

"No, what did you start to say?"

"Do you think we can go visit Brian tomorrow?"

"We can. That's a good idea. I want to see the little guy myself."

Karri smiled. "Good." She took a sip of her wine.

"You like kids, don't you?" Jake commented.

"I suppose. I've never really been around a lot of kids, but I like Brian."

Jake leaned over and kissed her. Her lips were cool and soft. He could taste the wine.

"I'm getting a little tired. Maybe we should go to sleep." She stood up. I'm going to go get changed."

"Okay. I'll pull the couch out and get the pillows and blankets."

Karri left the room leaving Jake sitting on the couch confused. Her abrupt suggestion about going to sleep made him wonder if she was anxious to sleep with him again or did she want to avoid it tonight. It was like the beginning of last night all over again.

He got up and removed the cushions and pulled open the couch into the bed. From his bedroom, he brought out the blankets and pillow but decided to leave his sleeping bag.

When he heard Karri come back into the room, he looked and found that she was not dressed in the sweatshirt and sweatpants like the last two nights, but instead she was wearing a short, thin silk nightshirt. He had his answer.

She slid under the blanket. "Joining me soon?"

"I'll be right back." He quickly went to the bathroom to wash up and was back in a few minutes to join her under the blanket for another night of lovemaking.

Sometime around two a.m., Jake felt Karri get out of bed and go into the kitchen. He heard the water faucet being turned on and knew she had got up for a drink of water. But then, he heard her talking. She had left her cell phone on the counter charging and was now talking on it. He listened.

"Brent, why are you calling me?"

Jake thought about getting up. He didn't like that her old boyfriend was calling her, but decided to listen for a little longer.

"Yes, I'm coming back home.... Soon. I have to get back to the store.... No, I haven't sold the farm yet, but I'm going to call the attorney this week and tell him to take the offer.... It's none of your business how much money I'm going to get for it.... I know you're sorry about what happened between us.... I'm not going to talk to you about us tonight. Do you know the time difference between Kentucky and California? It's the middle of the night here and I need to get back to sleep.... All right, I promise to call you when I get back. Goodnight."

Jake felt a lump in his throat. She was selling the farm and going back to California. What was even worse, she sounded like she might reconcile with her old boyfriend. How could she sleep with him and within a few hours promise to call Brent when she returned? Well, if that's what she wanted, that was fine with him. With any luck, the power will be back on and she can go back to the farm tomorrow.

He heard her come into the room and crawl back into bed. She snuggled close to him and he didn't move.

CHAPTER TEN

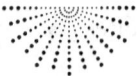

Karri woke up late the following morning. She reached over to the other side of the bed but found it empty. Jake had probably already gone to the barn to take care of the animals. She went into the bathroom to change clothes and realized that the overhead light was on. She picked up Jake's electric razor that was plugged in and turned it on. It worked. The power had been restored.

"Karri?" She heard Jake calling from the kitchen and went in to meet him.

"The power is on," she said.

"Yeah, it was on when I got up this morning. I can take you back to your house whenever you're ready."

She was a little taken back by what seemed like his anxiousness for her to leave. "How about some breakfast?"

"Sure. I already made some coffee before I went to the barn."

Karri got a cup from the cabinet and poured herself a cup. She took a sip and put the cup on the counter so she could start breakfast. "Bacon and eggs okay?"

"Yes." Jake went into the laundry room to wash his hands. He also opened the door to let Colt back inside.

Karri got the food from the refrigerator and started frying. "Could we go see Brian before taking me back to the house?"

"I think Brian would like that."

She quickly got breakfast dished up and they ate in silence. Karri was puzzled at Jake's behavior. He wasn't acting like someone who had shared a bed with her.

When she finished eating, she cleared her dishes and took them to the sink. Jake finished and did the same thing. "Don't bother with the dishes. I'll do them later," he said.

Again, more strange behavior. "Okay. I'll just pack my clothes and we can get going."

Twenty minutes later, Jake put her bag into the backseat of his truck and Colt jumped in afterward. Karri climbed in the front and they drove to Tim and Renae's to see Brian.

"I put some can goods and stuff in a box in the backseat so you would have some food to fix until you can get your car out to go to the store."

"Thanks. I appreciate that."

When they arrived at the farm, Tim greeted them at the door. "Welcome, please come in." He closed the door behind them after they entered, followed by Colt. Tim took their coats. "Renae and Brian are in the kitchen, go on in."

Remembering the way, Karri took the lead and entered the kitchen.

"Miss Karri!" Brian shouted in excitement and ran over to her.

"Hi Brian, how are you?" Karri kneeled down and gave the little boy a hug.

"Oh, I'm fine. Did you know I took a helicopter ride?"

"I know. How was that?"

"Well, I don't really remember it, but the pilot came and saw me at the hospital and said I could come see the helicopter when I got better. I'm better now, but mommy won't let me go." He rubbed Colt's head.

"Brian, I told you that you could, but not yet," Renae said. "Why don't you take Uncle Jake to your room and show him all the things you brought home from the hospital?"

The boy's eyes lit up. "Come on, Uncle Jake. I'll show you the toy helicopter I got when I woke up at the hospital." He took Jake by the hand and practically dragged him out of the kitchen with Tim following.

Renae looked at Kari. "You wouldn't believe all the toys and things he got while there. Please, sit down. Would you like some coffee? I just made it."

"Yes. Thank you." She took a seat at the table.

Renae got up to get the coffee. "How are things with you and Jake?"

"What?"

"Oh, maybe I shouldn't have said anything. Tim came home from Jake's and said that you two were in a relationship now. I just assumed it was okay to ask."

"That's fine. I'm not really sure what you would call what we have."

Renae brought their coffee to that table and sat down. "What's wrong?"

"I never should have slept with him. I knew I would be going back to California, but I did it anyway."

"Did you let Jake think you were going to stay here?"

"No. I told him right from the start that I couldn't stay, but he didn't care and damn those deep brown eyes of his." The ladies laughed.

"Now that you've fallen for him, you don't want to say goodbye, right?"

"Something like that." Karri took a sip of coffee. "I knew it was wrong to get involved."

"You needed each other. He's been alone for a long time."

"Before coming here, I had just broken up with my boyfriend."

"Maybe you should consider staying here in Kentucky. You already have a house," Renae suggested.

"But, I have a business to run back home. I wish I could stay here, but it's just not possible. I even checked into how much it would cost to renovate the farmhouse into a bed and breakfast. It was so much more than I could afford." She took another sip of coffee. "I decided yesterday that I'm going to tell my attorney to accept the offer he got on Aunt Alma's farm."

"The offer from that company in Louisville? You know what they'll do to the farm."

"I do know. I wish there were another way, but I don't have any other choice."

Renae walked to the counter and brought a plate of cookies to the table. "When will you leave?"

"In a few days, depending on what papers I need to sign for the sale." Karri picked up a cookie, dipped it into her coffee, and took a bite.

"I'll miss you. You've become a good friend in the short time you've been here," Renae said.

"I'll miss all of you."

Jake, Tim, and Brian came back into the room.

"Mommy, can I go outside and play in the snow?" Brian asked.

"I think you played in the snow enough the other day. You need to stay inside and keep warm for a while."

"But, the snow is gonna melt today," he pleaded.

"Brian, listen to your mother," Tim said.

Karri looked up at Jake. "Don't you think we should get me home? I need to see if there was any damage to the house from the blizzard."

"We should, and I still have to dig your car out too," Jake added.

Karri stood, as did Renae. The two ladies hugged. "I'll stop by before I leave town," Karri whispered to her friend. "Brian, you be careful when you play outside."

"I will."

Karri and Jake put their coats on at the front door and said their goodbyes before going out the door. "It looks like he's recovered nicely," she said.

"He's just as hyper as ever," Jake said.

He opened the truck door for her to get in and then got in on the driver's side. He started the engine and headed for Alma's farm.

Tim had done a good job plowing the road to the farmhouse. Jake had no trouble getting down the drive. He parked out front and helped Karri out. She carried her bag of clothes and Jake carried the box of food into the house. Colt jumped out of the truck behind them.

"Colt, wait here," Jake ordered.

"He can come in."

"No, he needs to stay out."

They walked inside.

"It's warm in here," Karri said.

"When the power came back on, so did the furnace," Jake explained. He took the groceries into the kitchen and sat them on the counter. "I'm going to turn the water back on at the main switch. Can you go upstairs to the bathroom and make sure nothing is leaking when I turn it back on?"

"Yes." She took her bag of clothes and headed upstairs to do as he said. She went into the bathroom and waited. In a short time, water started coming out of the sink and the bathtub faucets. She turned both of them off and then checked the pipes for any leaks. With everything looking fine, she went back downstairs.

Jake was in the downstairs bathroom checking the pipes down there when she stood at the door. "Everything is okay upstairs," she said.

"It looks good down here too."

She stepped back to let him by her and go back out into the living room.

"I'm going to go dig your car out. Can I have the keys?" he asked.

She got the keys from her purse and handed them to him. "Can I help with anything?"

"No, I can do it quicker alone. You should probably get the milk and eggs in the refrigerator."

"You're right. I should probably do that." She turned and went to the kitchen and heard him close the front door as he went out. After getting the groceries put away, she got her cell phone out and called Alex in California.

"Hello."

"Hi, Alex. It's Karri."

"I was just thinking about you."

"Really? What were you thinking?"

"That you should be coming home soon."

"I am, probably in a few days."

"I saw Brent today, and he said he talked to you last night. He really misses you."

"I told him he and I would talk when I got back." She grabbed a kitchen towel and began wiping the dust off the counter.

"I was afraid you might have decided to stay in hillbilly country."

"Don't call it that, Alex. These people aren't like that. They're friendly, caring, and loving."

"I'm sorry. Is everything okay with you?"

"I really messed up. I fell in love with Jake and then slept with him."

"What's wrong with that?" Alex asked.

"I let my guard down when I shouldn't have. I can't stay here. What was I thinking when I slept with him? My life is in California, not Kentucky."

"Whoa, Karri. Slow down. Did something happen?"

"Not that I can remember. Last night, we had a wonderful dinner, went to bed and then this morning, he acted differently to me. He seemed more distant than before."

"Did you tell him you decided to sell and come back to California?"

"No, not yet. I'm really dreading that conversation."

"He probably has a lot on his mind and didn't even realize he wasn't paying attention to you."

"Maybe. Will you be able to pick me up at the airport when I get back?"

"You know I can."

"Thanks. I'll call when I have my flight information. I'm going to meet with the attorney tomorrow and see what I have to do for the property sale. After that, I'll get my flight reservations." Karri heard the front door open. "Alex, I have to go. Jake's coming into the house. I'll call later. Bye." She ended the call and walked into the living room.

"I got your car dug out from the snow and moved it," Jake said, handing her back the keys to the car. "It's warming up outside, and I think you'll be able to get out whenever you want."

"Thank you. Would you like some coffee to warm you before you go?"

"No, thanks. I have a lot of things I need to do at my farm."

"Of course, I should have thought of that."

Jake turned toward the door to leave.

"Thanks for rescuing me from the storm. I don't think I could have survived here at the house alone."

Jake turned to her and chuckled a little. "You would have done just fine. You're a survivor. You would've figured something out."

"Well, thanks anyway. I appreciate all you've done for me while I've been here."

"You're welcome. If you have any problems, call me." He turned to the door and walked out.

Karri felt like she had been stabbed in the heart and it was all her fault. She heard his truck engine start and pull away from the house. At the window, she watched him drive up the driveway and finally out of sight. She sat on the couch and thought about her situation. She was a strong woman, and she would survive another heartache. She had her life and friends in California, and the sooner she got back home, the better. She picked up her cell phone and dialed.

"Gilmore Law Office. Can I help you?"

"This is Karri Taylor. May I speak to Mr. Gilmore?"

"One moment, please."

She listened to the elevator music play while waiting.

"Hello, Miss Taylor. How can I help you?"

"Mr. Gilmore, I've decided to accept the offer on my aunt's farm, if they're still interested."

"I'm sure there's still some interest in the purchase. I will make some calls today and get back to you."

"That would be fine. Please do so as soon as possible. I'm anxious to get back to California as soon as I can."

"Can you come into my office to sign some paperwork and I'll contact the buyer. Was the last price they offered still acceptable for you?"

"Yes."

"Very good."

"I can probably come in as soon as I can get my car out."

"That would be fine. No need for an appointment, just stop by."

"Thank you, Mr. Gilmore. I'll see you in a little bit." She ended the call.

Before going into town, Karri needed to make a list of things she would need to do before going back to California. She would have to clean the house again, so more cleaning supplies went on the list. She looked through the kitchen to see if there were any other groceries she needed. She also would have to make arrangements to donate Aunt Alma's furniture too.

After making a short shopping list, she went upstairs to change clothes. When she came back down, the clock on the wall that showed two-thirty and she needed to get to town. She put on her coat, picked up her keys and purse and walked out the door. She said a silent prayer that she could get the car out of the driveway. Thankfully, Jake had moved it so it already pointed in the right direction. The sun was shining and it seemed even brighter out with the reflection from the snow, which felt a little slushy under her shoes. She got in and started the engine, putting it in gear she pressed on the gas pedal. At first the tires spun in the snow, but then gained traction and the car started forward. She drove slow and steady until she got to the top of the little hill and only occasionally felt her tires spin. She drove past Jake's driveway and briefly looked that way thinking she might see him on the tractor, but there was no sign of him.

Soon, she reached the highway, which was clean and clear of snow and ice. Once in town, she looked for a place to park near Gilmore's office. Snow piled as high as cars were all along the sides of the street with no parking available. She finally found the town parking lot and turned into it. Thankfully, it had been cleared of snow. Dirty mounds of snow bordered the lot with only a few breaks in the walls to walk through. She parked as close as she could to Gilmore's office and started her walk through the wall of snow. The sidewalks were clear, but it was a strange feeling walking behind the wall of snow from the street.

She entered Gilmore's office and wiped her feet before going into the waiting area. His secretary sat at her desk, dressed a little more casual than before. Her snow boots sat on some newspapers on the floor next to her desk. "Miss Taylor, right?"

"Yes, Mr. Gilmore told me I could stop by anytime today to sign some papers."

"He's expecting you. If you'll come with me, I'll take you right in." She stood, and Karri followed her into Gilmore's office where he was on the phone. He hung up immediately when he saw her.

"Miss Taylor, please come in and sit down." He stood.

She took a seat in front of his desk and he sat down also. The secretary closed the office door as she left.

"I have some good news for you. Right after you called, another buyer called to make an offer on the farm, an even larger offer," he said.

"More than the one from the company from Louisville?"

"Much more." He handed her a copy of a purchase agreement.

She looked at the form. "Well, that is good news. I assume you accepted it?"

"Not yet."

"I don't understand."

He sat up straighter in his chair. "I think it's only fair to speak with the first bidder to see if they want to make a higher offer."

"Who is the second buyer?"

"I don't know. A realtor from Lexington contacted me with the offer. All they would say is it was from a private individual."

Another mysterious buyer, she thought.

"I really think we need to contact the first company before any offer is accepted," he urged.

"Mr. Gilmore, I don't want to turn this into a bidding war. Please accept this second offer and proceed with the sale. I wasn't happy about selling to that company in Louisville anyway after hearing what they wanted to do with Aunt Alma's farm."

"No one knows for sure if it's the same company that's buying up all the area farms."

"No one knows they aren't either."

"I just think---"

"Accept the offer Mr. Gilmore and call me when you have the paperwork ready for my final signature. I emailed you my bank account number for the deposit before I came in." She stood. "I want to leave for California as soon as possible." She turned and walked out of the office.

She was happy with the offer on the farm and hoped it was from someone who would not, in turn, sell it to the other company for a profit. Before leaving town, she stopped by the store to pick up the items on her list. She needed to start getting things at the house ready to close it up.

The grocery store had its own parking lot, and when she pulled in, she saw Jake's truck parked by the front door. She eased in next to it and shut the off engine. She got out and started toward the front door when Jake walked out carrying a big bag of dog food. "Hello," she said.

"Hi," he responded. "I'm glad to see you got out. Did you have any trouble?"

"No, and thanks again for digging me out and turning the car up the hill."

"You're welcome."

"Looks like Colt will be eating good tonight."

"Yeah, I forgot to get his food when we were out last time."

Both stood there in silence for a few seconds.

"Well, I better get going," he finally said.

"Yes, that looks heavy."

He stepped past her and put the bag of dog food in the back of his truck. When he turned back toward her, she turned away and went inside to get her supplies.

She spent all of the next day cleaning the farmhouse. Most every-thing had already been disposed of when she first arrived in

Kentucky, but she had accumulated a few things while she was there. Late in the day, her cell phone rang.

"Hello."

"Miss Taylor?"

"Yes, this is Karri Taylor."

"This is Tammy Kent, James Gilmore's secretary. He wanted me to tell you that the paperwork for the farm sale to the buyer from Lexington is ready to sign. Could you come into the office sometime tomorrow afternoon to finalize the sale?"

"Yes, I can. I didn't think it would happen so fast."

"Apparently, the buyer is anxious to take possession. If you could come in around noon, I should have all of the paperwork ready, and all we'll need is your signature."

"I'll be there. Thank you."

Karri tapped her phone to end the call and went to her laptop to make a reservation for a flight back to Los Angeles. The first available flight left the next evening at five p.m. That should give her enough time to sign the paperwork, drive to the airport and drop off the rental car. Of course, that meant getting back to California in the middle of the night. She hoped Alex wouldn't mind picking up that late.

She picked up her phone and dialed.

"Hello."

"Alex, it's Karri. I have my flight information. I'm coming back home tomorrow."

"That's great. When will you be in?"

"My flight arrives at twelve a.m. I hope you don't mind picking me up that late."

"No, I can do that, but do you mind if Andy comes with me, so I won't be alone?"

"That's fine, just don't bring Brent."

"Oh no, I wouldn't do that."

Karri knew that was exactly what was going through Alex's mind. "Okay, I'll see you then. Thanks."

"Bye, Karri."

The two ladies hung up. She had packing to do.

Karri tossed and turned all night finding it hard to sleep, and by six in the morning, she was wide awake. I might as well get up, she thought. With plenty of time before she was to arrive at the attorney's office, she decided to take a long bath. One of the things she loved the most about her great-aunt's farmhouse was the clawfoot bathtub and she wanted to enjoy it one more time. She turned the hot water on in the bathtub and poured some lavender scented bath oil into the tub and used her hand to mix it into the water. She breathed in the aroma. Removing her clothes, she turned off the water and stepped into the tub sliding down into the water. The twenty-minute soak in the tub made her feel like a new woman. She dried off and dressed before going back downstairs, she looked around the bathroom and bedroom to make sure everything was packed and then carried her bags downstairs.

After making some toast and coffee, she emptied the contents of the refrigerator and tied up the trash bag. She would put it out in the trash can for the garbage pickup later in the day. While in town earlier in the week, she had stopped by Aunt Alma's church to make arrangements for the furniture to be picked up and then delivered to a family that could use it.

Looking at the clock on the wall, Karri sat at the kitchen table to write a note to Jake. She planned to stop by to see Renae before she left for her teaching job at the school. She wanted to talk to Jake before she left, but knew if she did, she'd break down into tears. She wanted to keep that from happening, so she'd leave a note with Renae for him.

It was difficult for her to find the words that she wanted to say to him. Finally, she finished it and slipped it into an envelope. As a last-minute thought before sealing the envelope, she put a business card from her bookstore inside. She had just enough time to catch Renae at home before she left for school.

She got in her car and drove to Renae's. She arrived at the home and knocked on the door. In a few seconds, Renae answered.

"Karri, what are you doing here so early?"

"I wanted to stop and say goodbye. I sold the farm and am leaving this afternoon to go back to California."

"Oh, my. Please come in." She stepped back so Karri could come in and closed the door behind her. "Can I get you some coffee?"

"No, thanks. I don't want to keep you from school."

"I don't need to leave for another thirty minutes. Come on into the kitchen. Brian's just finishing his breakfast."

She followed her into the kitchen.

"Hi, Miss Karri. What's ya doing here so early?" the little boy said from the kitchen table while slurping down some cereal.

"Hello, Brian. I just wanted to stop by to tell you goodbye. I'm going back to my own home in California."

"Where's Cal - Cali - forna?"

Karri couldn't help but chuckle at his attempt to say California. "It's a long way from here."

"You're gonna come back and visit, aren't you?"

The little boy's puppy dog eyes broke her heart as she tried to hold back a tear. "I'll try, sweetie."

"Brian, go wash your face and hands, we need to be going soon," Renae said.

The little boy got up and ran out of the room.

"Goodbyes are so hard," Karri said. "I'm glad I met you and Tim, and I'm going to miss you. Kentucky will always have a special place in my heart." She gave Renae a hug.

"I wish you were staying. It's been a while since I had a friend like you."

"Here's my card with my e-mail address on it. I hope you'll keep in touch."

"Of course, I will. Are you going to stop to see Jake before you leave?"

"I don't think so. It'd just be too hard. I wrote him a note, if you wouldn't mind seeing that he gets it." She handed Renae the envelope. "Please don't give it to him until tomorrow."

"I'll make sure he gets it," she promised.

Brian came running back into the room carrying his coat. "Mommy, are you ready to go?"

"I drop him off at my mom's while I'm at school during the day. I probably should get going."

"I need to do the same." The ladies walked to the front door and hugged. "Thanks for everything you did for me while I was here."

"You're welcome. I'm sorry it didn't work out between you and Jake, and I'll make sure he gets your note."

"Thanks." Karri turned and went to her car. She looked back at the house as she drove away, giving Renae and Brian a wave and then wiping a tear from her eye.

As she drove back to the farmhouse, she was amazed at how quickly the snow had melted since the blizzard. There were still a couple inches on the ground, but the roads were completely cleared and dry. She parked her car in front of the house and went inside. Time seemed to be moving so slowly, and she felt anxious to get everything over with. With only having toast and coffee to eat that morning, she decided to go into town for a proper breakfast. After loading her luggage into the car, she did one more walk through the home. Finally, she headed out, locking the door behind her, but before getting into the car, she took out her cell phone and took a photo of the house.

At the restaurant in town, she took as much time as she could to eat breakfast. After all the coffee she drank, she hoped her seat on the plane would be close to the restroom. She gave the waitress her credit card to pay the bill. She thought about returning to Willow Creek sometime for a visit, but then again, that might not be a good idea. By the time she could return, Jake would probably have a girlfriend, or maybe even a wife. No, that would be too hard.

The waitress returned, and Karri signed the credit receipt and left. It was early to go to Gilmore's office, but she would just as soon wait there as anywhere. A drive of a few blocks, she parked in the town parking lot again and followed the same path as she walked before to the office.

"Miss Taylor, you're early," the secretary said.

"Yes, I didn't have much else to do, so I thought I would come in and maybe get this over with."

"Mr. Gilmore just returned from court and he's on the phone with someone right now. He hasn't had lunch yet, but if you'll have a seat, I'll see if he can see you early."

"Thank you. I'd really appreciate that."

The secretary started typing something on her computer while Karri sat and waited. She hoped she could get in to see him soon. Her emotions were all over the place, and she needed to get to the airport before she changed her mind about leaving.

"Miss Taylor." James Gilmore stood at his door.

Karri stood and walked into his office. He closed the door behind her and they both sat down. "I'm sorry for showing up early. Your secretary said you haven't had lunch yet."

"It's fine and pretty common on most days. I have the paperwork ready for your signature." He handed her a file folder. "I have each line marked where you need to sign."

Karri opened the file, looked over the forms inside, and let out a deep breath. "That's a lot of money."

"It is. Look over the document closely and make sure everything is to your liking."

When she finished reading over the agreement, she picked up the pen on Gilmore's desk and signed on each marked line. She closed the file folder and handed it back to him. "I guess that's it."

"It is." He took the folder from her and got up opening his door. "Tammy, would you make a copy of this for Miss. Taylor?"

The secretary took the folder and Gilmore sat back down at his desk.

"I spoke with the minister of Aunt Alma's church yesterday to make arrangements for someone to pick up her furniture that I donated. He said someone would get it tomorrow and then drop the key off to you here."

"That would be fine."

"I guess you'll need these." She placed a set of keys on his desk just as the secretary came in and handed Karri a copy of the agreement and the other to Gilmore. "Thank you," Karri said, placing it into her purse.

"Miss Taylor, the money should be in your bank account by the end of the week. Make sure you speak with an accountant or your banker about how to handle the deposit," he suggested.

She stood. "I'll do that as soon as I get back to California."

Gilmore stood also. "You're leaving soon?"

"My flight leaves at five today." She extended her hand and they shook hands. "Thank you so much for helping me with this."

"It's been my pleasure. Please feel free to call me if you have any questions later."

She smiled and left Gilmore's office. Getting into her car, she drove out of town without looking back.

CHAPTER ELEVEN

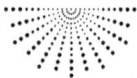

The alarm sounded next to Jake's bed. He hit the off button and sat up on the side of the bed. Five-o'clock seemed a lot earlier this morning than usual. Colt put his front paws on the bed and looked around. "Karri's not here," he told the dog, who then jumped back down and sat next to the bedroom door. "Okay, okay, give me a minute."

After going to the bathroom and dressing, he came back out going to the front door to let the dog out. "Scratch when you want back in." He closed the door and headed to the kitchen where the programmable coffee maker had just finished its brew cycle. Jake got his travel mug from the cabinet and poured himself a cup. After taking a drink, he sat it down and went to the laundry room to get his coat and boots on. He had to feed the animals. He grabbed his mug and headed to the barn.

The snow had melted on the trail he had taken to the barn the last several days. Colt followed in his tracks. Inside the barn, he lifted the top off of an aluminum storage can and put some dog food in Colt's bowl next to it. He picked up the pitchfork and started putting hay into the plastic bins in the corner of each stall for the horses to eat.

Jake had a lot on his mind. Things had ended poorly with Karri when he took her back to Alma's house. He should have told her that he overheard her talking on the phone with Brent. Maybe it wasn't as it sounded. After all, he'd only heard her side of the conversation. He loved her, and he didn't think she realized how much. Until now, he wasn't sure he even realized how much he loved her. He stopped what he was doing. He loved her. "I love her," he said out loud. He needed to see her, needed to tell her.

He heard the barn door open behind him and turned. "Hi, boss. How's everything this morning?" Marty, the farm manager, said.

"Marty, you got here just in time. Something has come up, and I need to go. Can you finish feeding the horses and then take the hay to the cattle out in the east pasture?"

"Sure, no problem."

"Oh, and the horses are going to need some fresh water too."

"I've got it. When will you be back?"

"Maybe later this afternoon," Jake called back as he went out the door.

Jake had taken Karri biscuits and sorghum on her first morning in Kentucky, and that's exactly what he would do again on this morning. While they baked in the oven, he quickly showered and shaved. He stepped back into the kitchen just as the oven timer went off. He took the biscuits out and put them in a basket lined with a towel and covered them. As he left the house through the laundry room door, he grabbed a jar of sorghum and drove to Karri's house.

The sun was up and shining brightly when he pulled up to the farmhouse and saw a big box truck parked in front. He got out of his truck and grabbed the biscuits and sorghum and went inside, where he found Randy Woodhouse and two other men from the church.

"Randy, what are you doing here?" Jake asked.

"Hey, Jake. Miss Taylor donated all of Alma's furniture to the church to distribute to needy families in the area."

"Donated?"

"Yeah, she sold the farm and went back to California. Didn't you know?"

"She's gone?"

"Yeah, I guess. All I know is that Reverend Campbell asked if me and the other guys would come and get all of the furniture here this morning. She didn't tell you she was leaving?"

"No, she didn't." He looked down at the ground. Why wouldn't she have said something, or at least goodbye? "You guys have breakfast this morning?"

The three men looked at each other and shook their heads no.

"Here, breakfast is on me." Jake shoved the basket of biscuits and jar of sorghum into Randy's hands and turned to leave.

He got in his truck and drove. "Why would she leave? It wasn't supposed to end like this." He picked up his cell phone and tried calling her. It went straight to her voicemail. He was at a loss for words and just hung up. He turned his truck onto Tim's driveway and drove up to his house. Standing at the front door, he used his fist to knock on the door.

A few seconds later the door opened and Renae stood there in her robe. "Jake, what are you doing here so early?"

"I'm sorry, but Karri's gone. Did you know she'd left?"

"Come in the kitchen. Tim is having breakfast. Would you like some coffee?"

"You knew, didn't you?" He stepped inside and followed her to the kitchen. "Renae, you knew she'd left and didn't tell me?"

They walked into the kitchen.

"Baby brother, what's going on?"

"Karri's gone back to California, and apparently, your wife knew she was going and didn't tell me."

"Jake, that's not fair," Renae said.

He looked at Tim. "I suppose you knew too."

"Let Renae explain."

He sat down at the table with his arms crossed over his chest and glared at Renae. "Explain."

"Karri stopped by here yesterday morning before I left for school. She said she sold Alma's farm and was on her way to town to sign the papers to finalize everything. Jake, she was heartbroken about leaving.

Selling that farm was probably the hardest thing she's ever done." Renae went to the counter to get the envelope Karri left.

"Why didn't you call me and tell me?"

"She asked me not to." She walked back over to the table and sat down. "She left this for you."

Jake took the envelope from Renae and opened it. He took the note out and read it.

JAKE, I'm sorry I didn't say goodbye in person, but it would have been too hard. Spending the last few weeks in Kentucky, and especially with you, was more than I could have imagined. It made my decision to sell the farm and go back to California so much more difficult. You're a remarkable man, and I will never forget you.

With love,

Karri

HE FOLDED the letter and put it back in the envelope. That's when he saw the business card from her bookstore inside.

"You okay, Jake?" Tim asked.

He cleared his throat. "Yeah, I'm fine. Renae, I think maybe I could use some of that coffee now."

She brought him a cup and sat it in front of him.

"I'm sorry about what I said," he told her. "You were only doing what she asked, and I respect that."

"What are you going to do now?" she asked.

"I don't know."

A knock came from the front door and Tim went to answer it. In no time, he came back into the kitchen followed by Deputy Wright."

"Joe here has something to tell us."

"I thought you all want to know that the State Police arrested James Gilmore last night."

"The attorney?" Renae asked.

"Yes, ma'am. He was involved with that big company in Louisville that's been trying to buy up all the farms around here," the deputy said.

"What's he charged with?" Jake asked.

"Fraud. He led folks to believe that he was working in their favor when actually he was working for that company to pay bottom dollar for the farms. He also admitted that the company was responsible for all of the vandalism and thefts that happened, even the arson at the Woodhouse's farm."

"That's amazing," Tim responded.

Jake just stared at his coffee.

"Well, I need to be going. I have to inform the other landowners. Oh, Jake, I stopped at Miss Taylor's farm, but they told me that she'd already sold it and left for California."

"Yeah, that's right."

"If you speak with her, could you tell her to call me? I need to see what she wants to do about the theft of her generator."

"Sure, Joe. No problem."

"Thank you all. I'll see my way out." The deputy left the kitchen.

"Wow, today sure is full of surprises," Tim said.

"I need to get ready for school." Renae left the kitchen.

"Are you going to call Karri about this?" Tim asked Jake.

"I don't know what I'm going to do yet." Jake took the last drink of his coffee and then left for home. He stopped by the barn and asked Marty to take care of the farm work today. Once he got to his house, he stayed inside all day and into the night. After dark, he sat on the couch with only the glow from the fireplace lighting the room. Colt sat at his feet and occasionally raised his head as if to check to make sure he was still okay.

He must have read Karri's note a hundred times trying to decide what it meant. One last time, he picked up her business card from the couch and looked at it. Pursing his lips tightly, he slightly shook his head up and down and got up. He walked to his desk and turned on the lamp. He rifled through the drawers until he found the phone book and started fingering through the yellow pages until he found what he was looking for and started dialing the phone.

"Yes, hello. I need to make a reservation for a flight to California for tomorrow."

***

Two days later

Jake arrived at the John Wayne Airport around three o'clock the next afternoon. Leaving the winter weather of Kentucky, the California heat hit him as soon as he stepped off the plane on to the walkway. He followed the others from his flight to the baggage pickup area, and after getting his bag, he went outside and took a taxi to the hotel where he had made a reservation.

Karri lived close to her bookstore in Costa Mesa, and that's where Jake had reserved a hotel room near there. The taxi dropped him off and he checked in and went to his room. It was almost five-o'clock when he decided to find the bookstore. He asked at the front desk and they told him where to find it. He stepped outside to walk to the store. He had no idea if she'd be there, but at least he would know where it was if he needed to go back tomorrow. Four blocks down the street, he turned the corner and stopped. The bookstore was across the street in front of him, and it was still open.

The traffic light changed, and he crossed the street. As he walked to the door, he looked through the windows to see if he could see Karri inside. There were too many people wandering around, and the windows were slightly tinted and covered with a lot of posters to see her inside. He stopped at the door and took a deep breath before opening it. He stepped inside and started walking around. The store was beautiful with shelves upon shelves of books and a small coffee café in the front corner. Karri had done a wonderful job with this store, and he was very proud of her.

"Can I help you? You look lost," the sales clerk asked.

Jake was startled at first. "Oh, yes. I'm looking for Karri Taylor. Is she here today?"

"Karri? No, I haven't seen her today. She just got back from a trip, and I don't think she will be here until tomorrow morning. You can check back then."

"Thanks. I will."

"Can I take a message letting her know you were here?"

"No. I'm an old friend and want to surprise her. Thanks, again."

Jake strolled out of the store and back to his hotel. As he walked, he almost felt a little relieved she wasn't there. He wasn't sure what how to tell her what he needed to say. In his room he turned the air conditioner on high and sat on the bed. He knew his anxiety would build all over again tomorrow when he returned to the store. He turned on the television and stretched out on the bed, tired, then realized how late it was in Kentucky and picked up the phone to order room service.

The next morning, with his body still on Kentucky time, he awoke very early and watched some television until it was time for the bookstore to open. Too nervous to eat, he skipped breakfast and a little after nine o'clock he made his way to the bookstore.

He went up to the counter where a young lady, different than yesterday, was working.

"Can I help you?" she asked.

"I was looking for Karri Taylor. Has she come in yet?"

"She opened the store this morning, but left just a few minutes ago to go to the bank. I don't expect her back until around lunch."

"I see. Thank you. I'll check back later." To say he was disappointed was putting it mildly. I guess when you own the place you can set your own hours, he thought as he left the store. On the sidewalk, someone handed him a flyer about an art fair being held in the park across the street, and he decided to go take a look.

Jake remembered Karri telling him that Costa Mesa had a blooming art community and he could see why. Everywhere he looked were artisans tending to their booths of wares. He spent most of the morning walking around looking at the items for sale. He made a mental note to come back later to get something to take home to Renae. She loved this kind of stuff.

On the street at the edge of the park, he saw a row of food trucks. The growls from his stomach reminded him that he hadn't eaten breakfast, but instead of eating, he decided to go see if Karri was at the store yet. Maybe she would join him for lunch.

He started to return to the store when he recognized the woman sitting on one of the park benches, not twenty feet in front of him. Karri sat there next to a man...Brent, no doubt. She was smiling and laughing. It looked like she was having a good time. He wanted to leave, but just stood there, not able to move.

Then Karri turned toward him. "Jake?"

"Hello, Karri."

She stood and walked over to him. "What are you doing here?"

Before Jake could say anything, Brent had stepped up behind her. "Yeah, Jake. What are you doing so far from the farm?" Brent taunted, putting his hand on Karri's shoulder. "Aren't your chickens missing you?"

She brushed his hand away and took a side step away from him. "Leave him alone, Brent."

"Oh, is the lady fighting your battles?"

"There's no battle between us, little feller. Unless you want to start something." Jake took a step forward, but Karri blocked his advance.

"He's not worth it, Jake." She turned to Brent. "Go home."

He pointed his finger at Jake. "Stay away from me, or you'll see how good our medical services are out here." He walked away.

Karri faced Jake. "I'm sorry about that."

"I can handle him."

She shook her head. "Boys will be boys, won't you? You didn't answer my first question, what are you doing here?"

He paused before answering. "I didn't get to say goodbye."

"I see." She looked down.

"Could we sit down and talk?" he asked.

She looked at her watch and then to him. "This really isn't a good time. I need to get back to the store for a meeting."

"How about dinner? I'm staying at the Mesa Inn, and there's a nice restaurant on the same street."

169

"The Greenleaf Café? Have you eaten there?"

"No, but it looked nice from the outside."

"It's a vegan restaurant. They don't serve meat or any meat by-products. I can't see you eating in a place like that." She chuckled. "I don't live too far from here. Why don't you come to my apartment tonight and I'll fix dinner? I owe you at least one dinner anyway."

"That sounds nice, and we'll talk then."

"We will." She pulled a small notebook from her purse and wrote something down, giving him the page she wrote on. "Here's my address. The hotel can probably tell you how to get there. How does seven sound?"

"Sounds fine. I'll see you then."

She stretched up and gave him a peck on the cheek. He watched as she quickly walked away. Her scent hung in the air, and he breathed it in. His growling stomach reminded him that he was hungry and dinner was still seven hours away, so he went back to the park to get lunch.

Jake didn't think seven o'clock would ever arrive, but at six-thirty, he stepped out of the hotel and started walking to Karri's apartment. He followed the directions the hotel clerk had given him and found her apartment. He knocked on the door.

"A few seconds later, Karri opened the door. "Hi, did you have any trouble finding me?"

He stepped inside. "No, not at all." He followed her inside. She looked beautiful. "Something smells good."

"It's all finished. It's in the oven warming. You do like Mexican food, don't you? I don't remember having it with you while in Kentucky."

"I love Mexican."

"Great. Come on in and sit at the table and I'll bring it out."

"Let me help." He followed her into the kitchen. He carried a bowl of Mexican rice out while she brought out a Burrito Casserole. They sat down to eat.

"This looks great," Jake said.

"Thank you."

During dinner, their conversation consisted of chit-chat about things back in Kentucky and places to visit while in California. After dinner, Karri and Jake took their wine into the living room and sat down on the couch. Jake brought the bottle for refills.

"You wanted to talk," Karri said. "What's up?"

"Deputy Wright stopped by to tell me that the company from Louisville that was buying up the farms was responsible for all the mishaps around, including the arson of the Woodhouse's farm and the theft of the generator at Alma's farm."

"Really? Wow."

"There's more. James Gilmore was working for the company so the farms would go for the lowest price possible."

"So, I got cheated?"

"Not exactly."

Before he could say anything else, she stopped him. "Jake, why are you really here? You could have told me all of this over the phone or in an e-mail."

"You left without saying goodbye, leaving me with just a note."

She took a sip of wine. "Like I said in that note, goodbyes are hard for me."

"Or, was it because you might have changed your mind?"

"I never thought Kentucky would affect me the way it did. I never thought I would meet someone like you."

"Then, why did you leave?"

"I have a life here. I have the bookstore."

"When you first opened your store, didn't you take a risk by doing that?"

"Yes."

"Why not take that risk again and sell the bookstore and move to Kentucky?"

"That's what I did," she said.

"What?"

She sat her wine glass on the table and turned toward him. "The meeting I had to get to today was to close the deal to sell the bookstore."

"You're coming back to Kentucky?"

"I guess I am."

He sat his glass down and stood pulling her up into his arms. "That's the best news I've heard in a long time."

"I was hoping to use the money from my sale to open a bookstore there."

"You don't have to do that," he said. "You can turn Alma's farm-house into a bed and breakfast, like you wanted."

She stepped back and sat back down on the couch. "Do you think I can get the farm back since Gilmore was fraudulent with the sale to that company?"

Jake sat down next to her and took her hand into his. "The farm wasn't sold to that company."

"Gilmore said there was a second buyer involved, but after you told me about his arrest, I just assumed that was some sort of real estate game to make sure that company got the farm."

"Karri, I bought Alma's farm."

She pulled her hand from his and sat there for a few seconds. Jake could tell she was trying to understand what he just said.

"You bought Alma's farm? Why?"

"I bought it for you---for us."

"Us?"

"Karri, I love you. I want to share my life with you, and I'm hoping you want to do that too." He reached into his pocket and brought out a ring. "This was my grandmother's ring."

She looked at it. "Did your late wife wear this ring?"

"No, she didn't want it. I always thought I'd give it to my son someday for his wife. I never thought I would fall in love again and I do love you."

"You bought Alma's farm. Why didn't you tell me?"

He laughed. "You didn't give me a chance. You just up and left. I was going to propose to you the next day and offer the farm back to you. Well? Do you accept my proposal?"

"Yes! Yes, I will marry you!" They both jumped up into an embrace.
"I love you, Karri."
I love you too, Jake."

The End.

ACKNOWLEDGMENTS

Thanks to everyone who answered questions from me about horses for this book. Special thanks to my husband for helping me figure out what the part of a horse barn is called that has the weathervane on it. By the way, it's a cupola.

ABOUT THE AUTHOR

Carol Preflatish lives in southern Indiana and shares a log cabin with her husband and two cats in what seems like an enchanted forest with a menagerie of wildlife constantly visiting. A few little-known facts about Carol are that she's a licensed amateur radio operator, has a degree in Physical Education, and is a collector of golf balls, shot glasses, and coins. Carol is a member of the Sisters in Crime organization and Kentuckiana Authors.

You can learn more about Carol's other books by visiting her web page at:

http://CarolPre.com